Lola's SUPER CLUB

"My Dad is a
Super Secret Agent"

PAPERCUTZ
NEW YORK

Lola's SUPER CLUB

1 - "MY DAD IS A SUPER SECRET AGENT"

Script and art
Christine Beigel + Pierre Fouillet

Original editors
Maxi Luchini + Ed

Original designer
Immaculada Bordell

© Christine Beigel + Pierre Fouillet, 2010
© Bang. Ediciones,2011,2013
contacto@bangediciones.com
All rights reserved.
English translation and all other editorial material
© 2020 Papercutz
English translation rights arranged through S.B.Rights Agency –
Stephanie Barrouillet

Paperback ISBN: 978-1-5458-0564-0
Hardcover ISBN: 978-1-5458-0563-3

Special thanks to Stephanie Barrouillet, Manu Vidal Ibañez,
and Eva Reyes

Papercutz books may be purchased for business or promotional use.
For information on bulk purchases please contact
Macmillan Corporate and Premium Sales Department at
(800) 221-795 x5442.

Jeff Whitman–Translator, Letterer, Production, Editor
Eric Storms, Ingrid Rios–Editorial Interns
Jim Salicrup
Editor-in-Chief

Printed in China
December 2021

First Papercutz Printing
Distributed by Macmillan

Lola's SUPER CLUB

"MY DAD IS A SUPER SECRET AGENT"

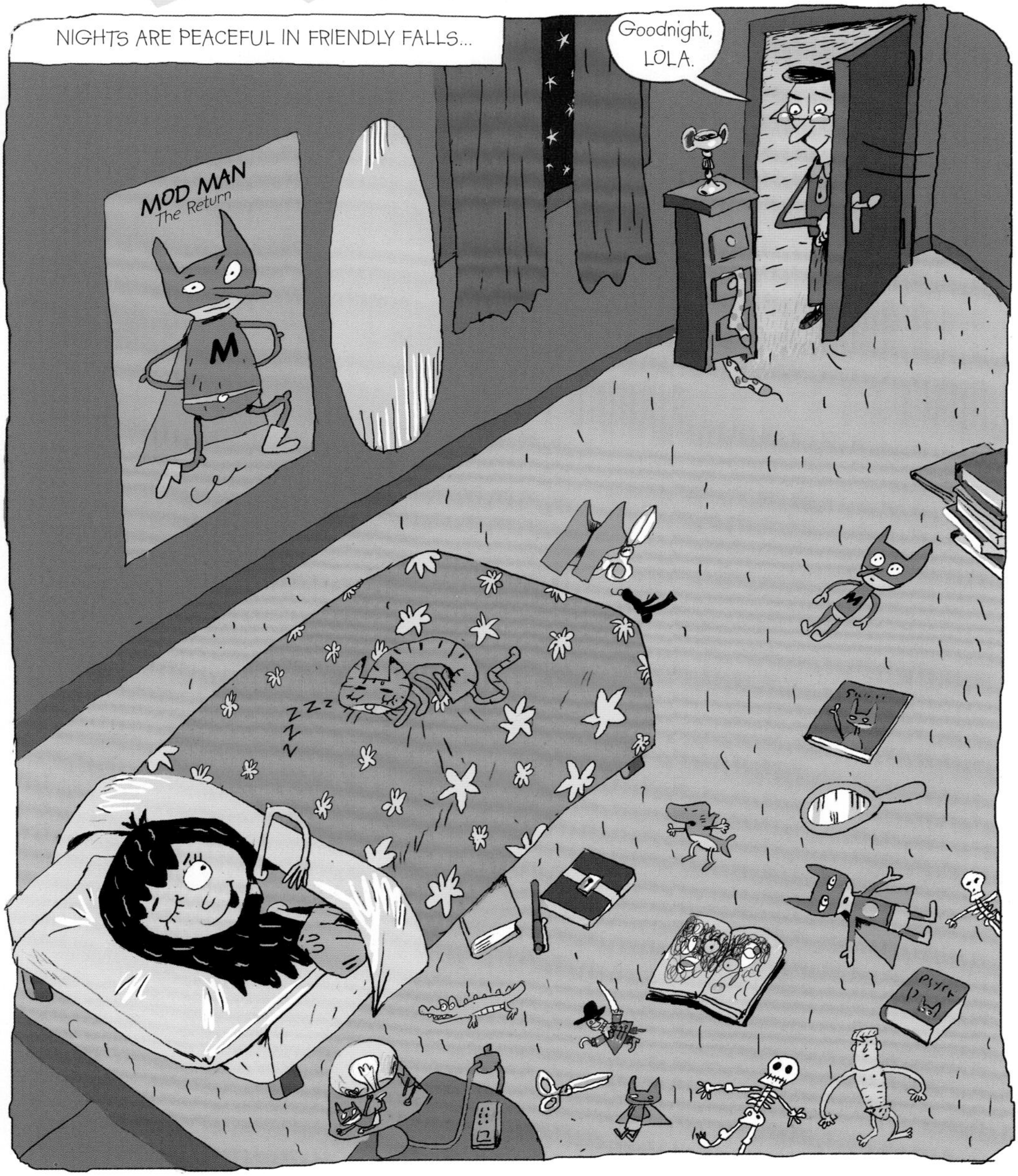
NIGHTS ARE PEACEFUL IN FRIENDLY FALLS...
Goodnight, LOLA.
MOD MAN
The Return
ZZZ
ZZZ

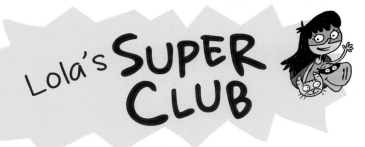

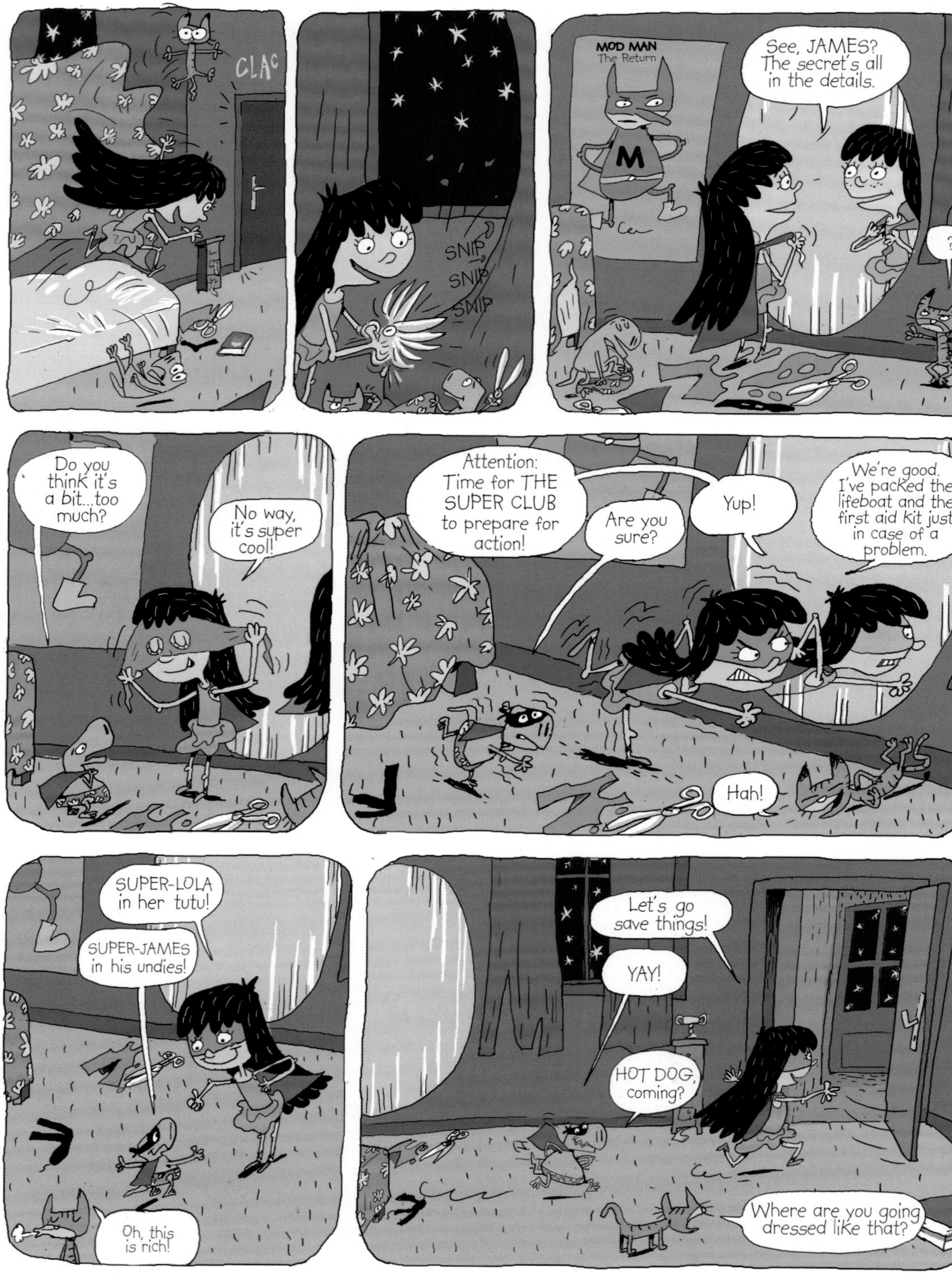
CLAC
SNIP
SNIP
SNIP
MOD MAN
The Return
See, JAMES? The secret's all in the details.
?
Do you think it's a bit...too much?
No way, it's super cool!
Attention: Time for THE SUPER CLUB to prepare for action!
Are you sure?
Yup!
We're good. I've packed the lifeboat and the first aid kit just in case of a problem.
Hah!
SUPER-LOLA in her tutu!
SUPER-JAMES in his undies!
Oh, this is rich!
Let's go save things!
YAY!
HOT DOG, coming?
Where are you going dressed like that?

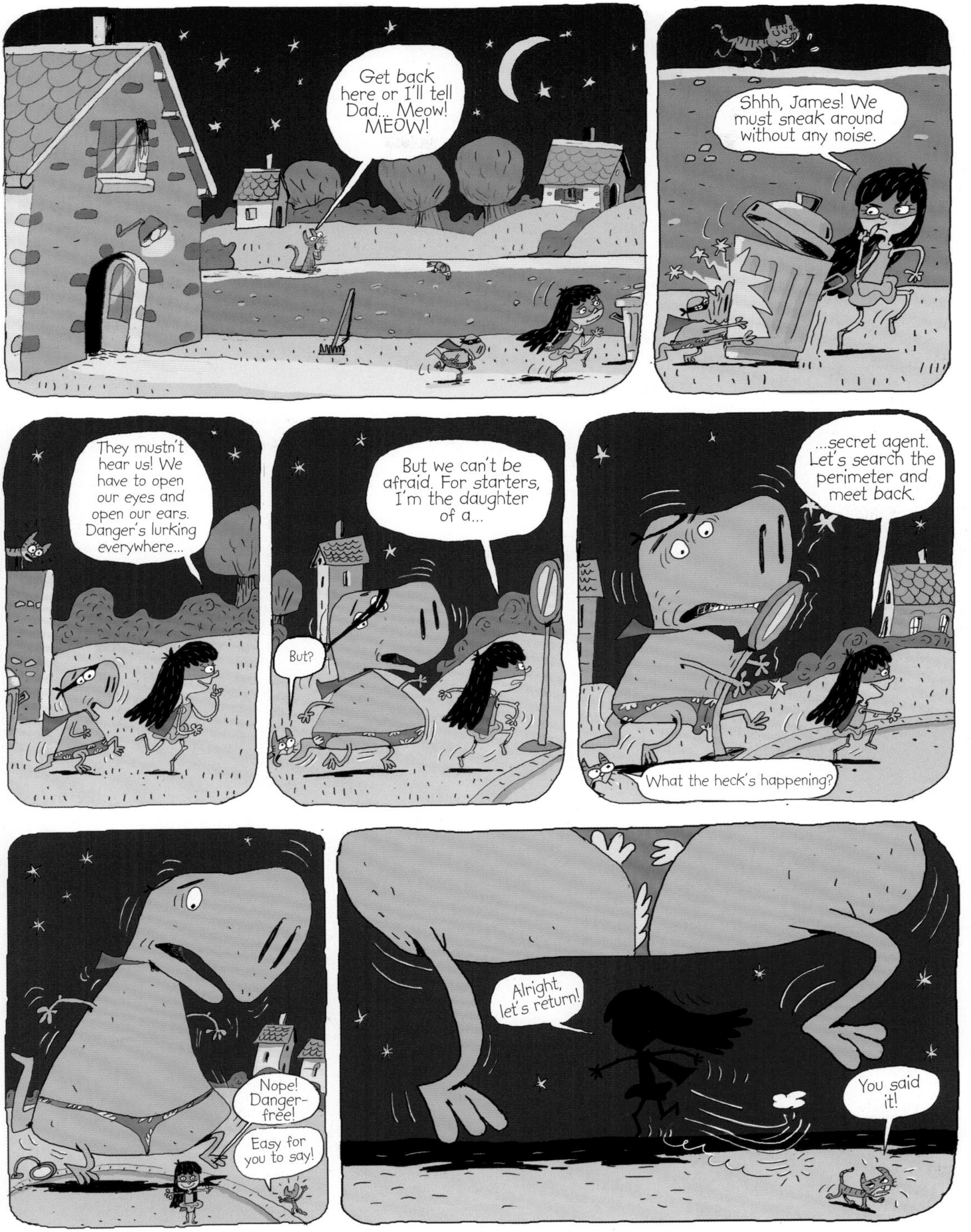
Get back here or I'll tell Dad... Meow! MEOW!
Shhh, James! We must sneak around without any noise.
They mustn't hear us! We have to open our eyes and open our ears. Danger's lurking everywhere...
But we can't be afraid. For starters, I'm the daughter of a...
But?
...secret agent. Let's search the perimeter and meet back.
What the heck's happening?
Nope! Danger-free!
Easy for you to say!
Alright, let's return!
You said it!

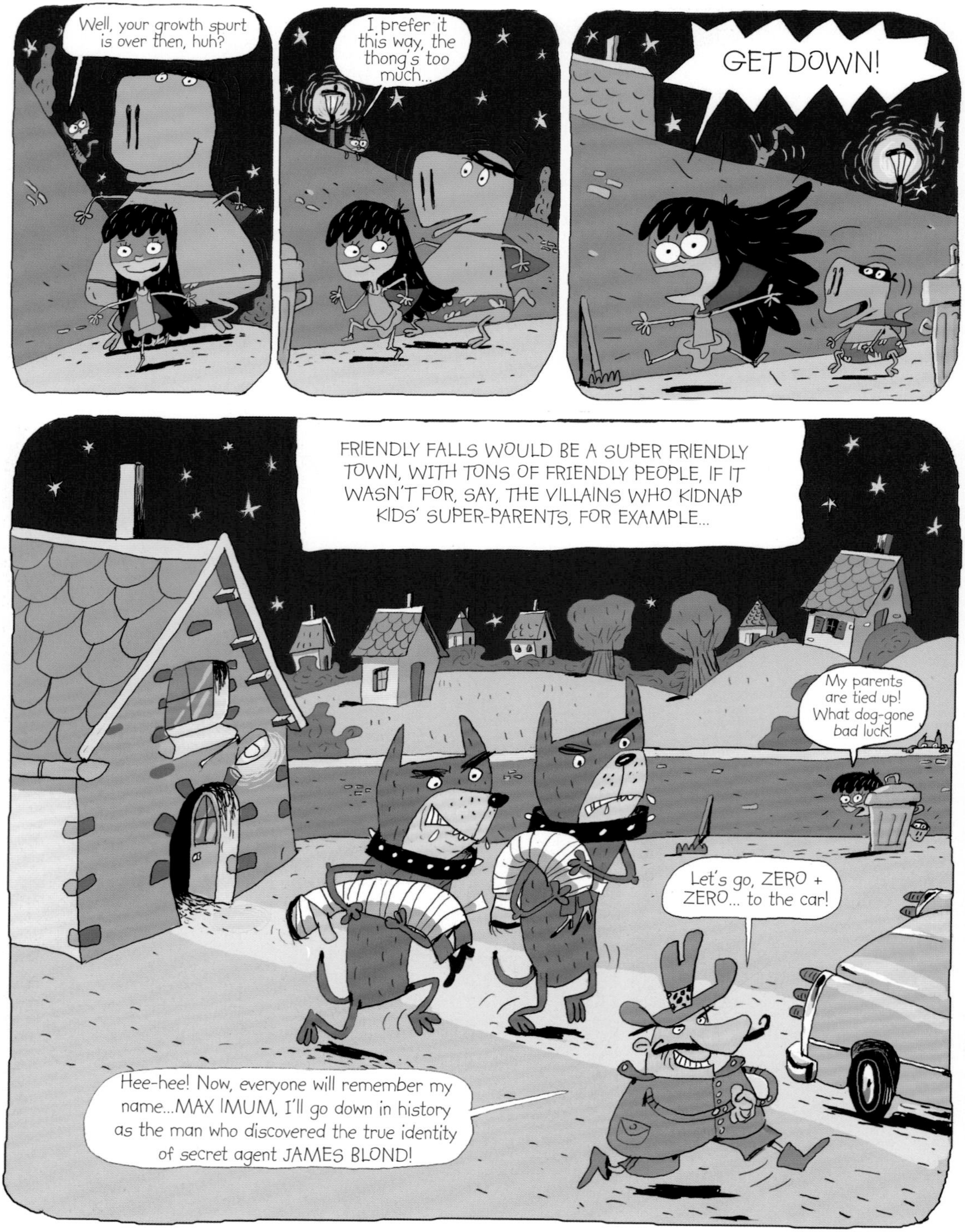
Well, your growth spurt is over then, huh?
I prefer it this way, the thong's too much...
GET DOWN!
FRIENDLY FALLS WOULD BE A SUPER FRIENDLY TOWN, WITH TONS OF FRIENDLY PEOPLE, IF IT WASN'T FOR, SAY, THE VILLAINS WHO KIDNAP KIDS' SUPER-PARENTS, FOR EXAMPLE...
My parents are tied up! What dog-gone bad luck!
Let's go, ZERO + ZERO... to the car!
Hee-hee! Now, everyone will remember my name...MAX IMUM, I'll go down in history as the man who discovered the true identity of secret agent JAMES BLOND!

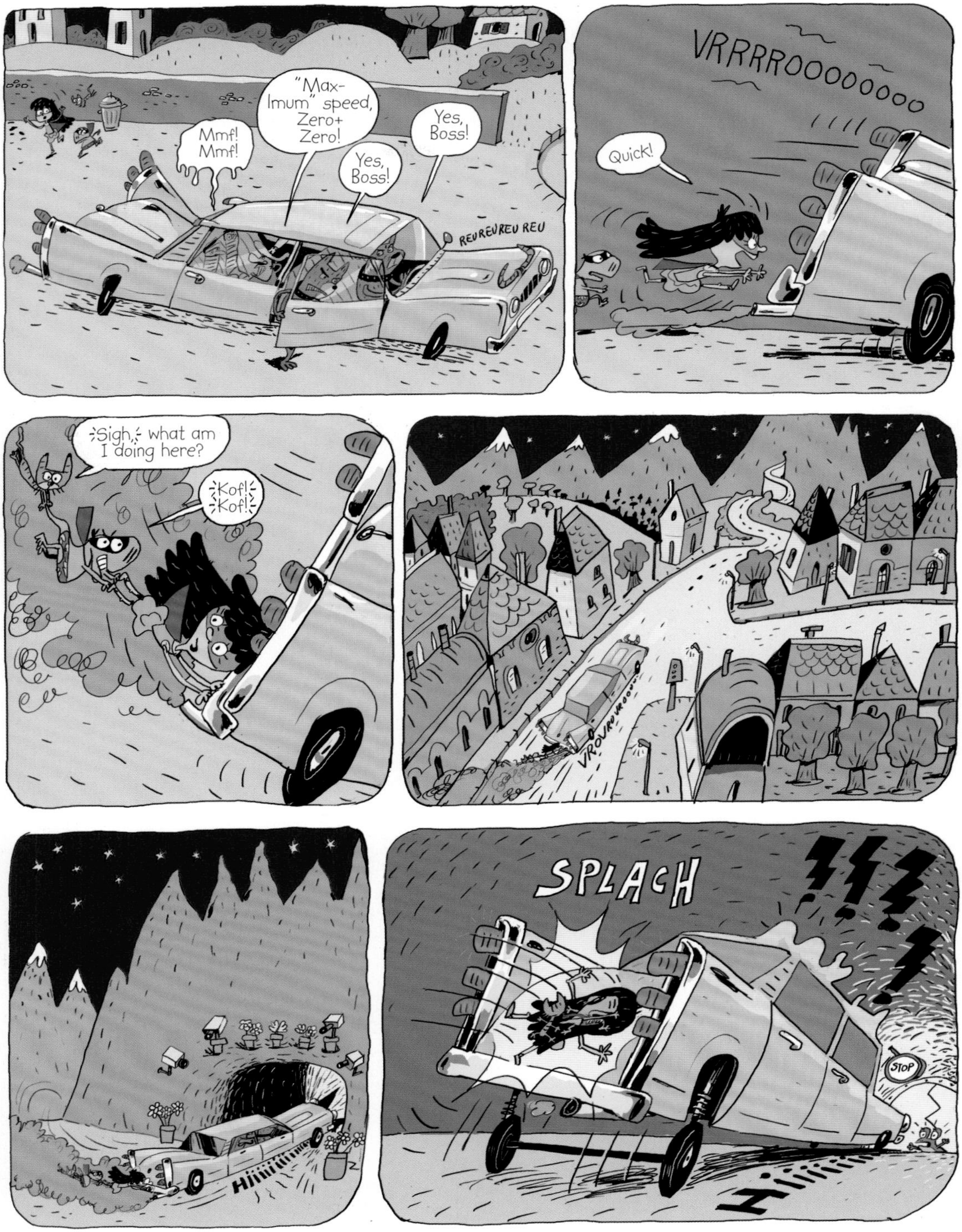
Mmf! Mmf!
"Max-Imum" speed, Zero+ Zero!
Yes, Boss!
Yes, Boss!
REUREUREU REU
VRRRROOOOOOOO
Quick!
Sigh, what am I doing here?
Kof! Kof!
VROUVROUVROOO
HIIIIIIIIII
SPLACH
STOP
HIIIIIIIII

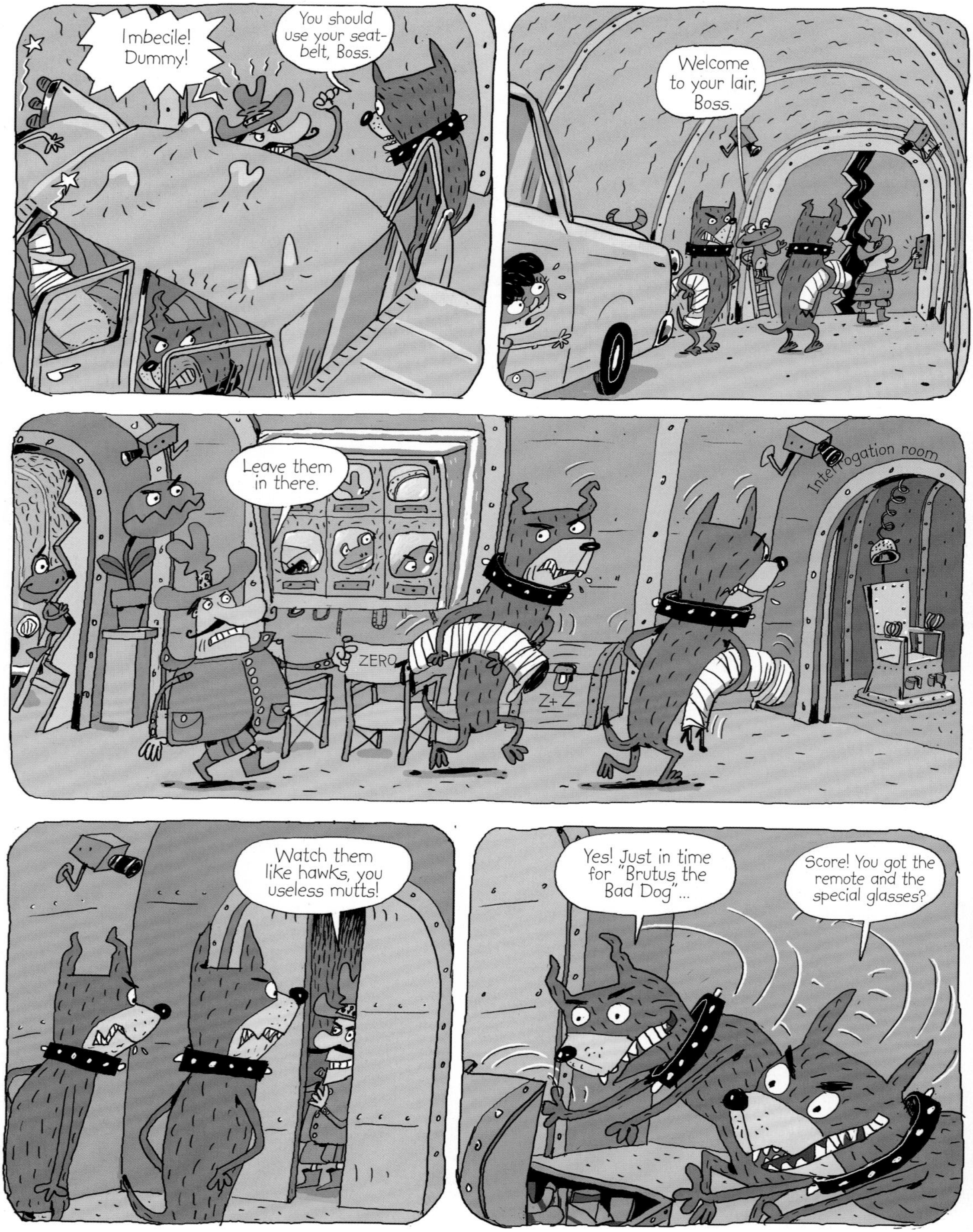

Imbecile! Dummy!
You should use your seat-belt, Boss.
Welcome to your lair, Boss.
Leave them in there.
ZERO
Z+Z
Interrogation room
Watch them like hawks, you useless mutts!
Yes! Just in time for "Brutus the Bad Dog"...
Score! You got the remote and the special glasses?

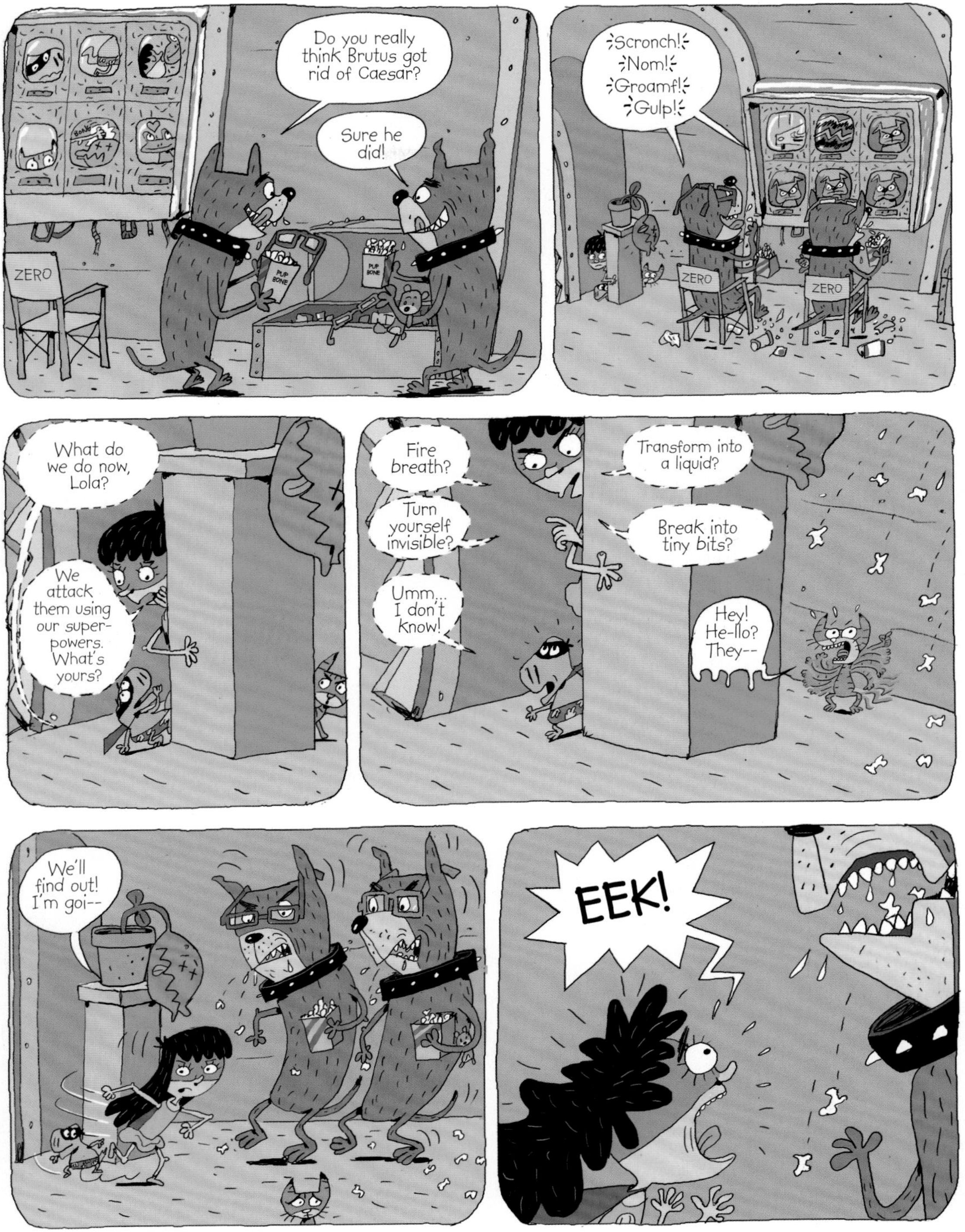
Do you really think Brutus got rid of Caesar?
Sure he did!
PUP BONE
PUP BONE
ZERO
Scronch!
Nom!
Groamf!
Gulp!
ZERO
ZERO
What do we do now, Lola?
We attack them using our super-powers. What's yours?
Fire breath?
Turn yourself invisible?
Umm... I don't know!
Transform into a liquid?
Break into tiny bits?
Hey! He-llo? They--
We'll find out! I'm goi--
EEK!

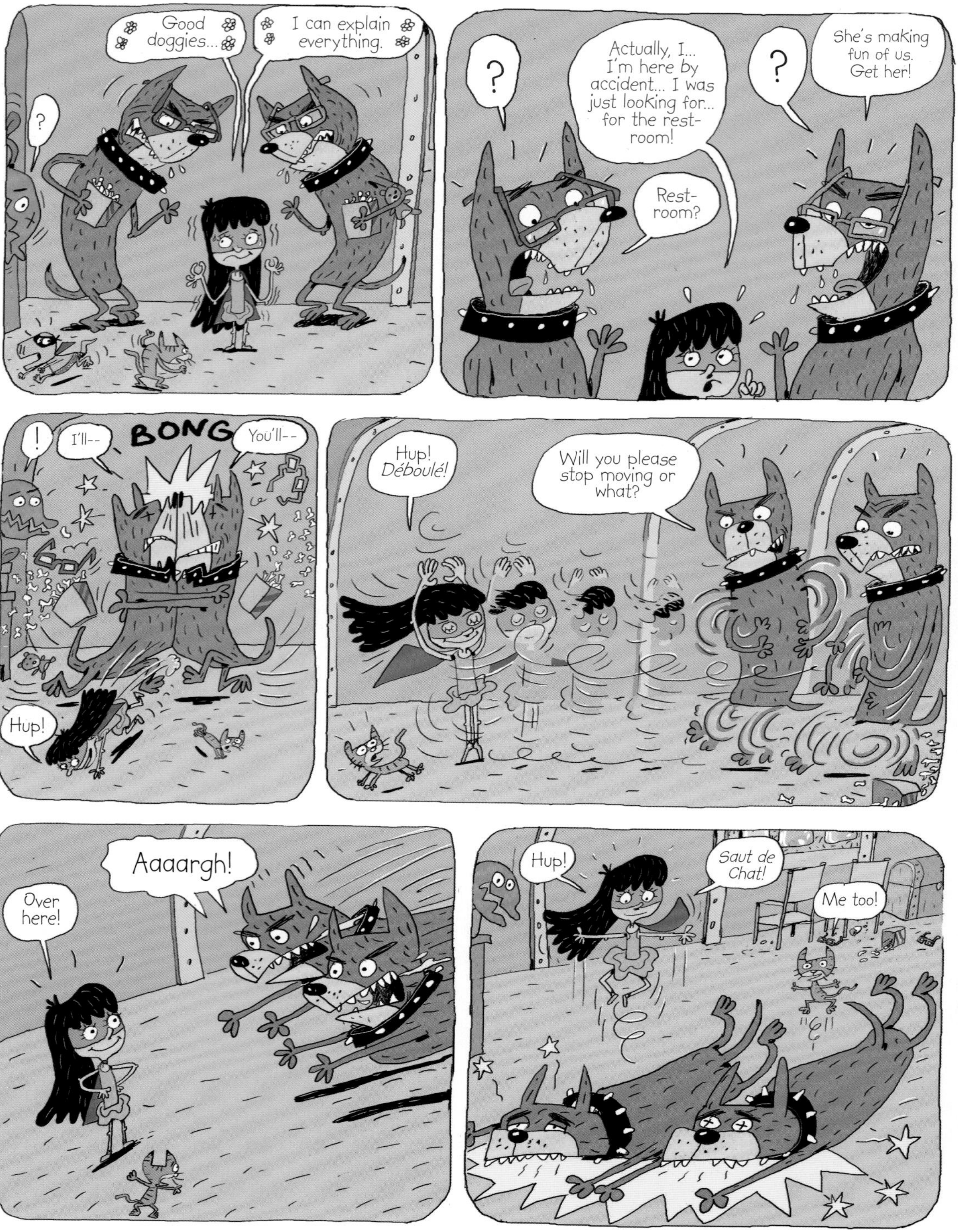
?
Good doggies...
I can explain everything.
?
Actually, I... I'm here by accident... I was just looking for... for the rest-room!
Rest-room?
?
She's making fun of us. Get her!
!
I'll--
BONG
You'll--
Hup!
Hup! Déboulé!
Will you please stop moving or what?
Over here!
Aaaargh!
Hup!
Saut de Chat!
Me too!

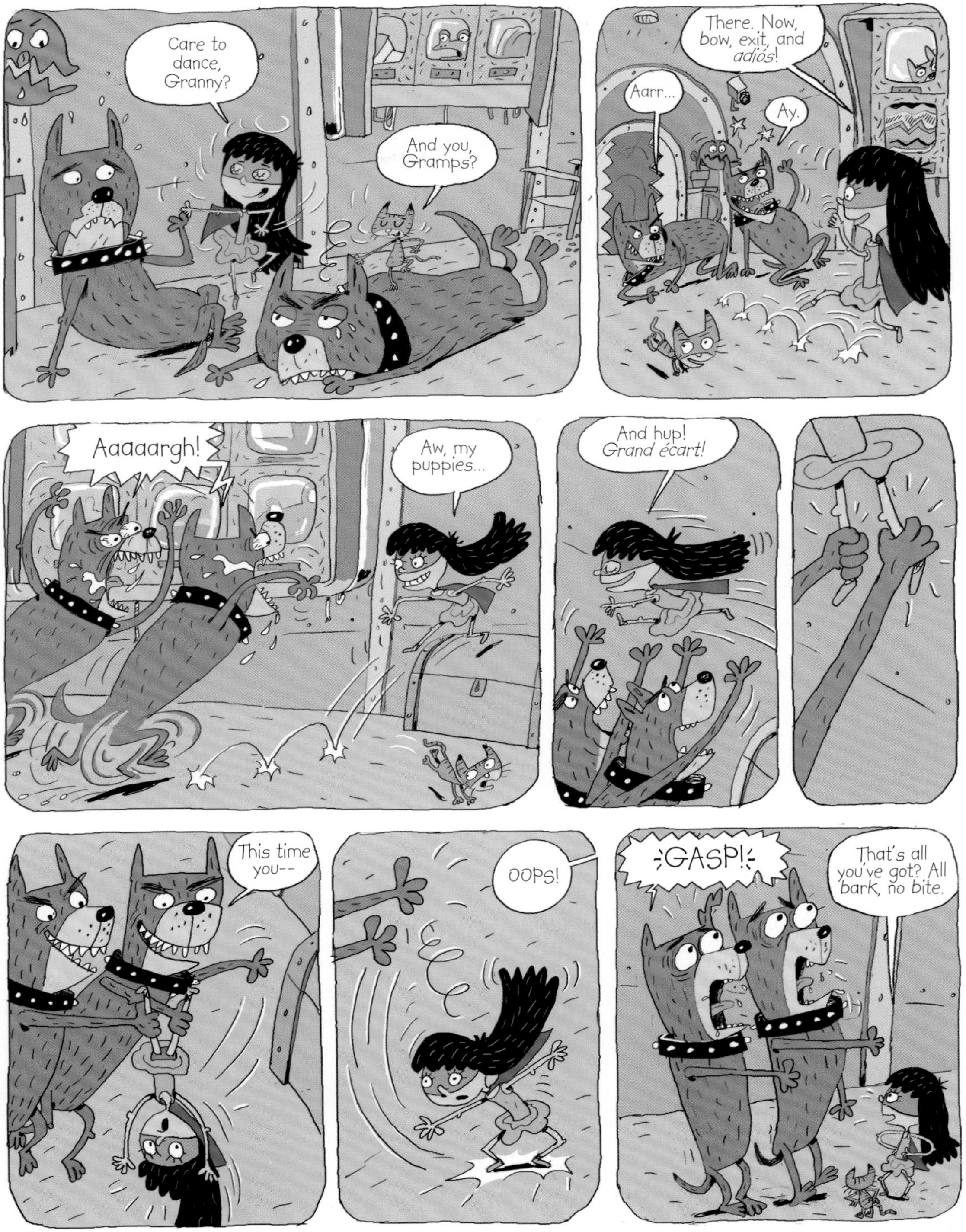
Care to dance, Granny?
And you, Gramps?
There. Now, bow, exit, and *adiós*!
Aarr...
Ay.
Aaaaargh!
Aw, my puppies...
And hup! *Grand écart!*
This time you--
OOPS!
GASP!
That's all you've got? All bark, no bite.

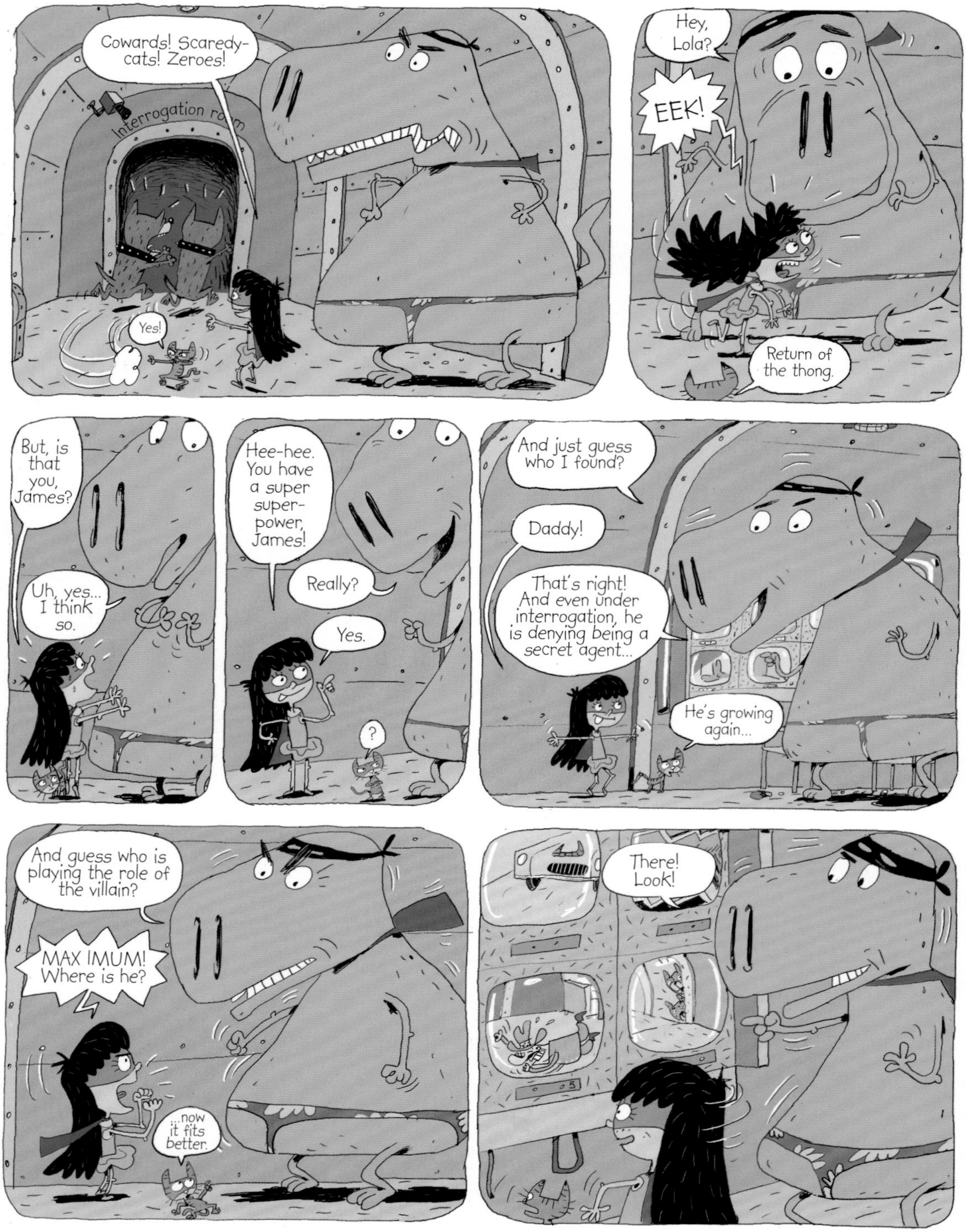
Cowards! Scaredy-cats! Zeroes!
interrogation room
Yes!
Hey, Lola?
EEK!
Return of the thong.
But, is that you, James?
Uh, yes... I think so.
Hee-hee. You have a super super-power, James!
Really?
Yes.
?
And just guess who I found?
Daddy!
That's right! And even under interrogation, he is denying being a secret agent...
He's growing again...
And guess who is playing the role of the villain?
MAX IMUM! Where is he?
...now it fits better.
There! Look!

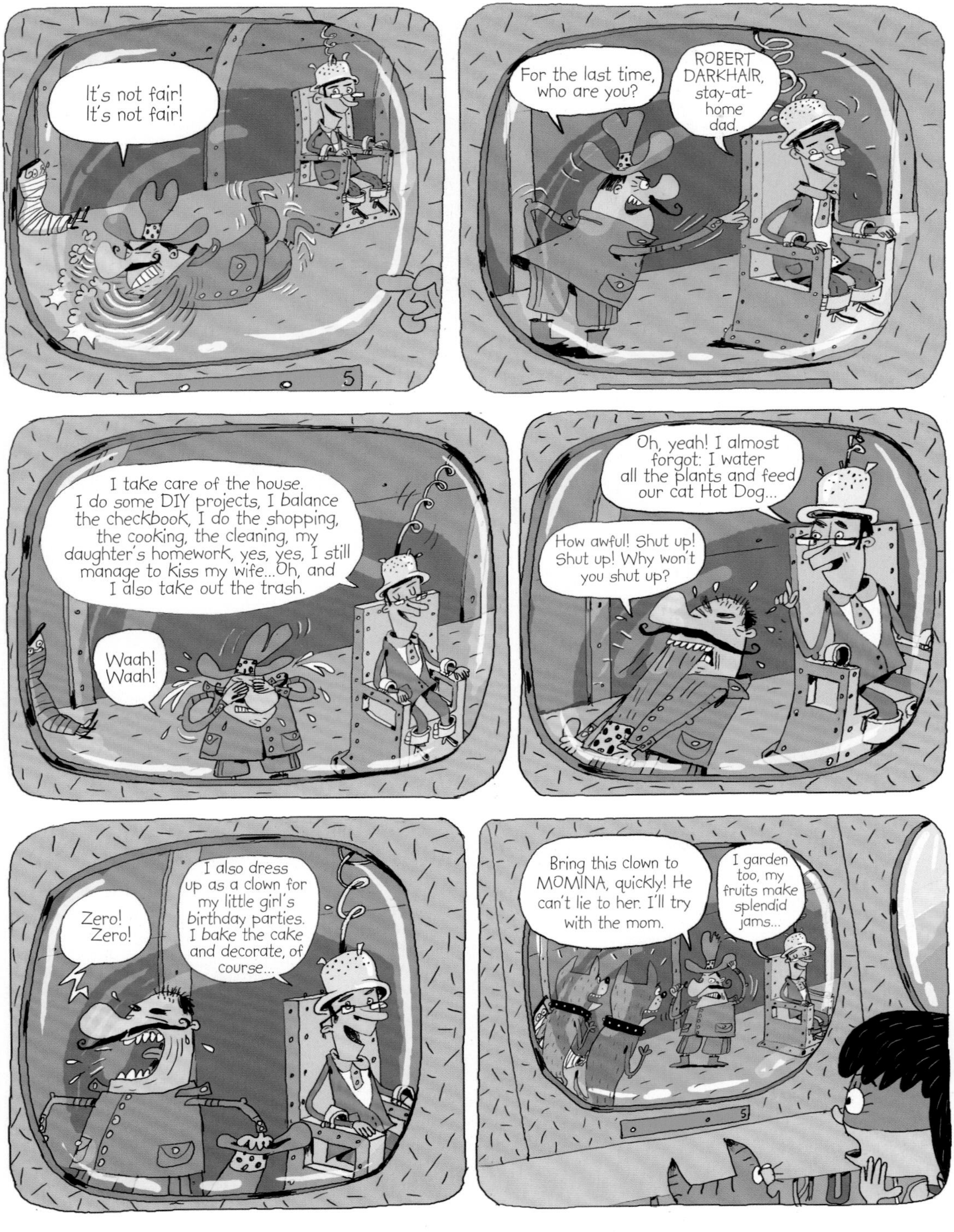
It's not fair! It's not fair!
5
For the last time, who are you?
ROBERT DARKHAIR, stay-at-home dad.
I take care of the house. I do some DIY projects, I balance the checkbook, I do the shopping, the cooking, the cleaning, my daughter's homework, yes, yes, I still manage to kiss my wife...Oh, and I also take out the trash.
Waah! Waah!
Oh, yeah! I almost forgot: I water all the plants and feed our cat Hot Dog...
How awful! Shut up! Shut up! Why won't you shut up?
Zero! Zero!
I also dress up as a clown for my little girl's birthday parties. I bake the cake and decorate, of course...
Bring this clown to MOMINA, quickly! He can't lie to her. I'll try with the mom.
I garden too, my fruits make splendid jams...
5

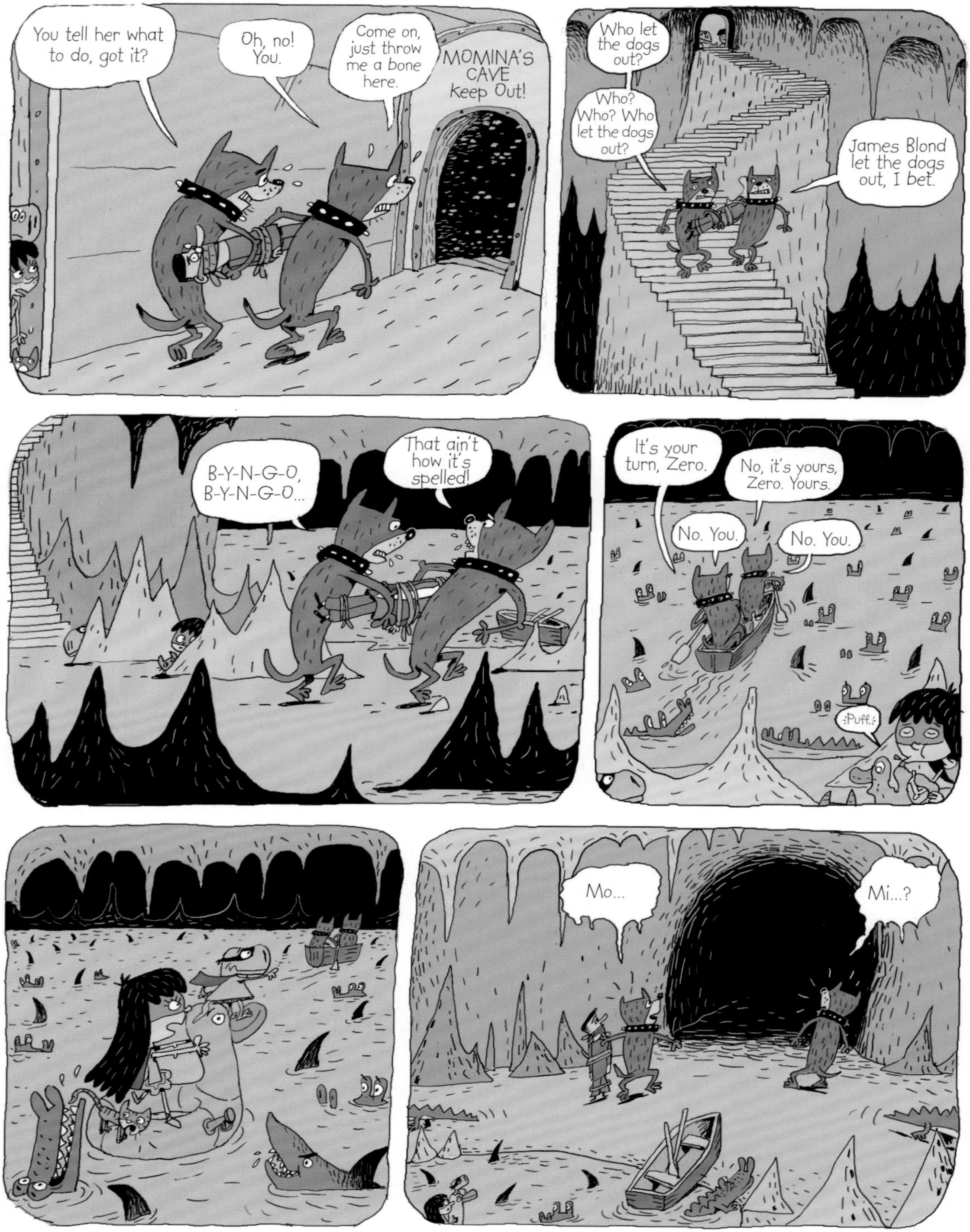

You tell her what to do, got it?
Oh, no! You.
Come on, just throw me a bone here.
MOMINA'S CAVE Keep Out!
Who let the dogs out?
Who? Who? Who let the dogs out?
James Blond let the dogs out, I bet.
B-Y-N-G-O, B-Y-N-G-O...
That ain't how it's spelled!
It's your turn, Zero.
No, it's yours, Zero. Yours.
No. You.
No. You.
Puff.
Mo...
Mi...?

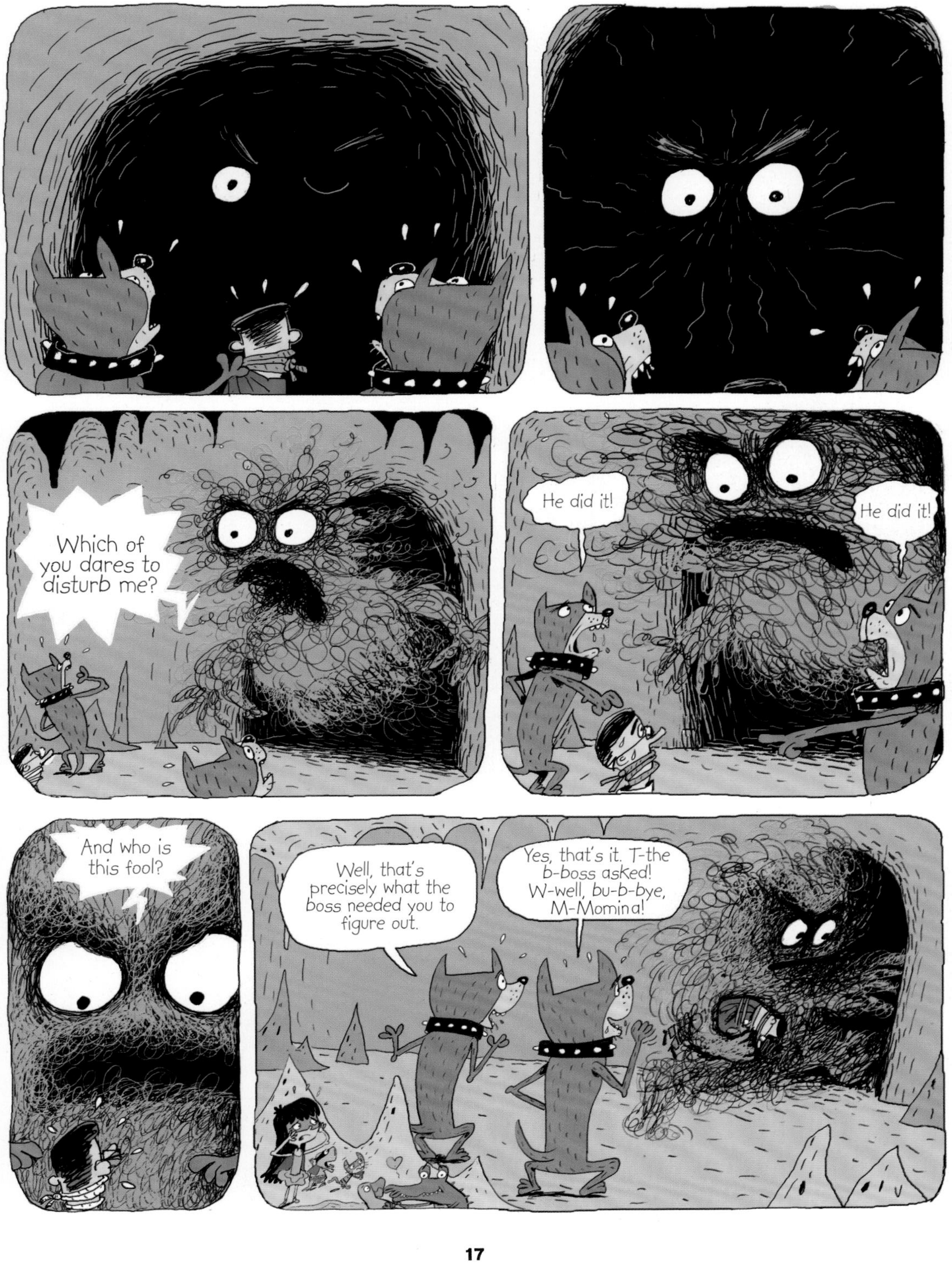
Which of you dares to disturb me?
He did it!
He did it!
And who is this fool?
Well, that's precisely what the boss needed you to figure out.
Yes, that's it. T-the b-boss asked! W-well, bu-b-bye, M-Momina!

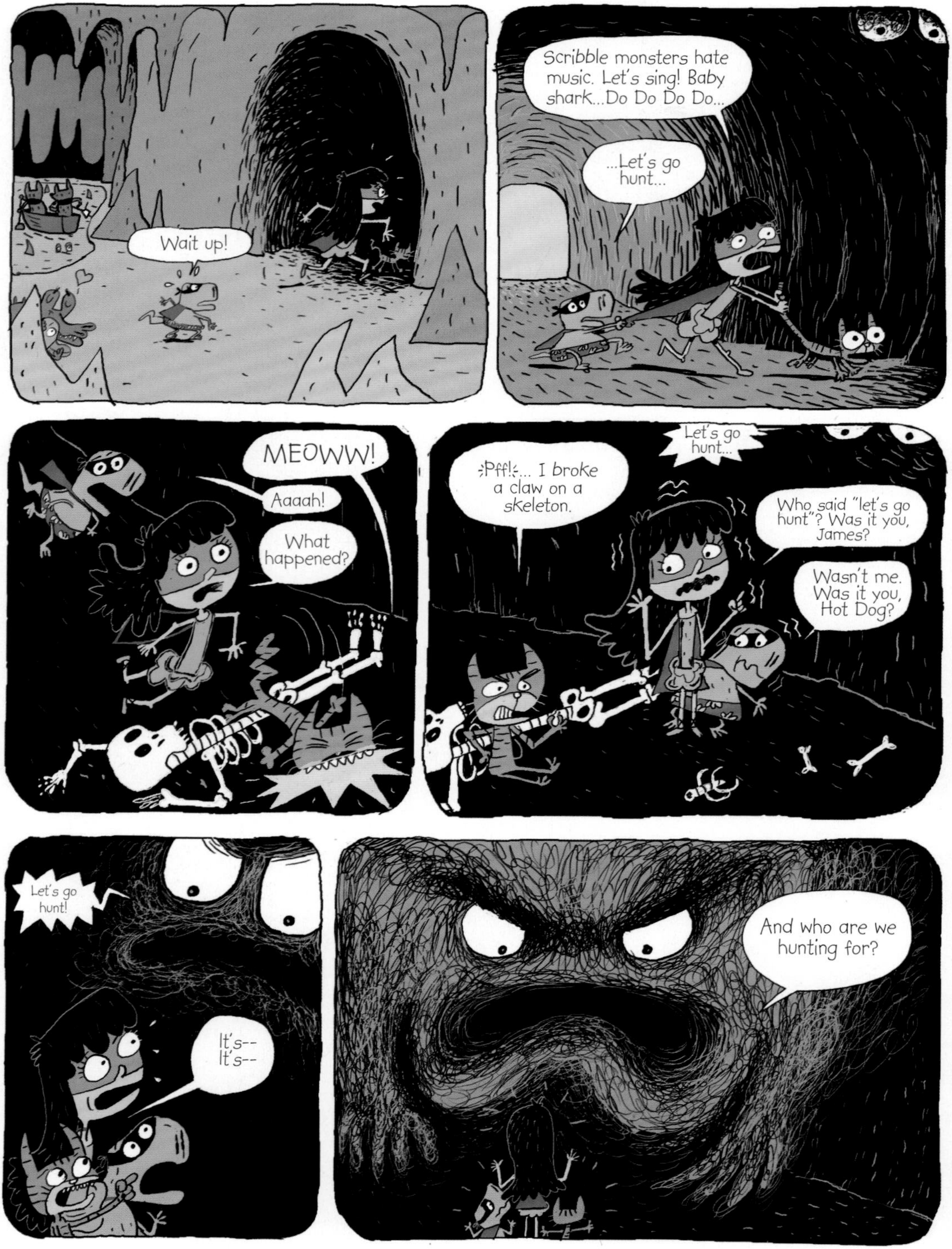
Wait up!
Scribble monsters hate music. Let's sing! Baby shark...Do Do Do Do...
...Let's go hunt...
MEOWW!
Aaaah!
What happened?
Let's go hunt...
Pff!... I broke a claw on a skeleton.
Who said "let's go hunt"? Was it you, James?
Wasn't me. Was it you, Hot Dog?
Let's go hunt!
It's-- It's--
And who are we hunting for?

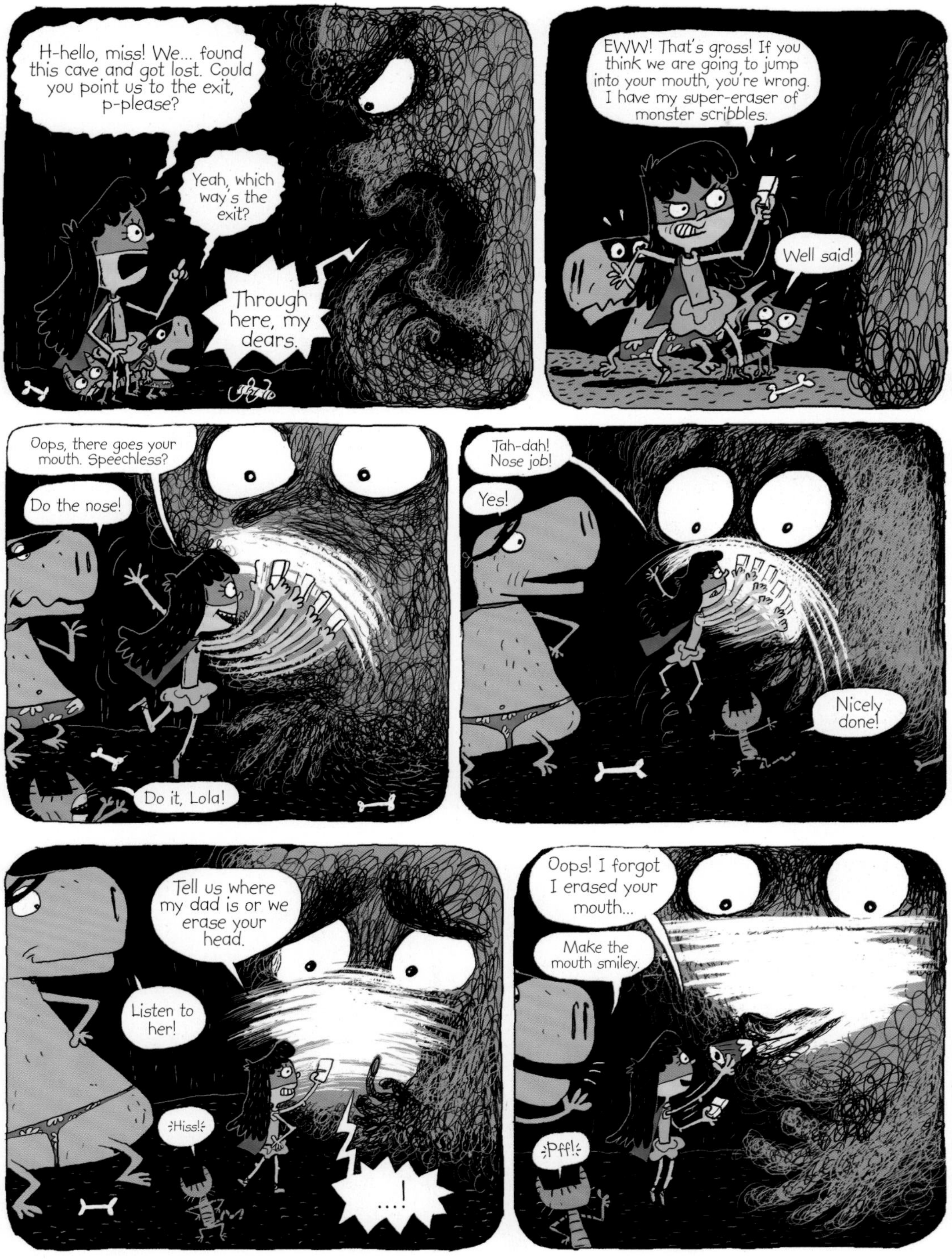
H-hello, miss! We... found this cave and got lost. Could you point us to the exit, p-please?
Yeah, which way's the exit?
Through here, my dears.
EWW! That's gross! If you think we are going to jump into your mouth, you're wrong. I have my super-eraser of monster scribbles.
Well said!
Oops, there goes your mouth. Speechless?
Do the nose!
Do it, Lola!
Tah-dah! Nose job!
Yes!
Nicely done!
Tell us where my dad is or we erase your head.
Listen to her!
Hiss!
...!
Oops! I forgot I erased your mouth...
Make the mouth smiley.
Pff!

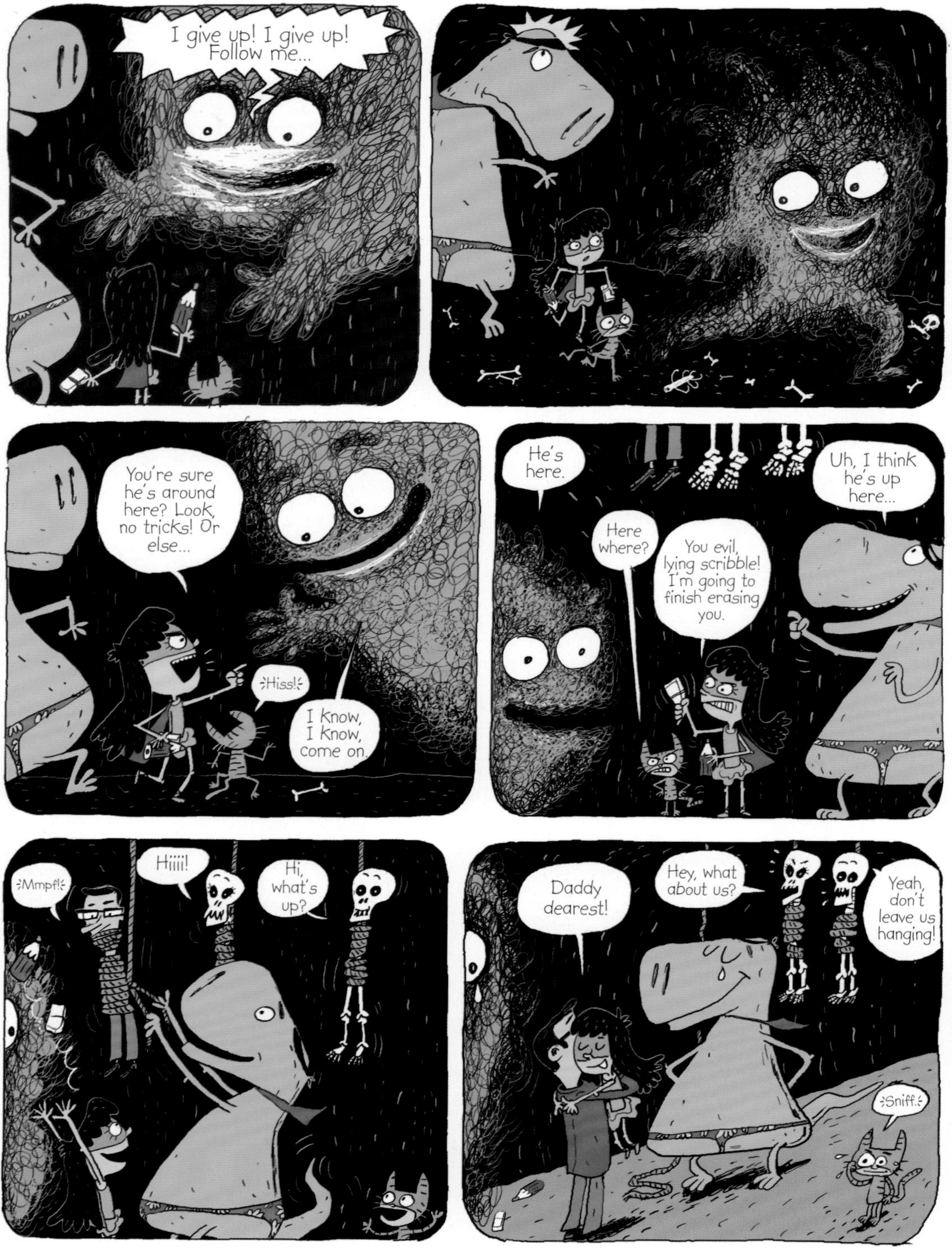

I give up! I give up! Follow me...
You're sure he's around here? Look, no tricks! Or else...
Hiss!
I know, I know, come on.
He's here.
Here where?
You evil, lying scribble! I'm going to finish erasing you.
Uh, I think he's up here...
Mmpf!
Hiiii!
Hi, what's up?
Daddy dearest!
Hey, what about us?
Yeah, don't leave us hanging!
Sniff.

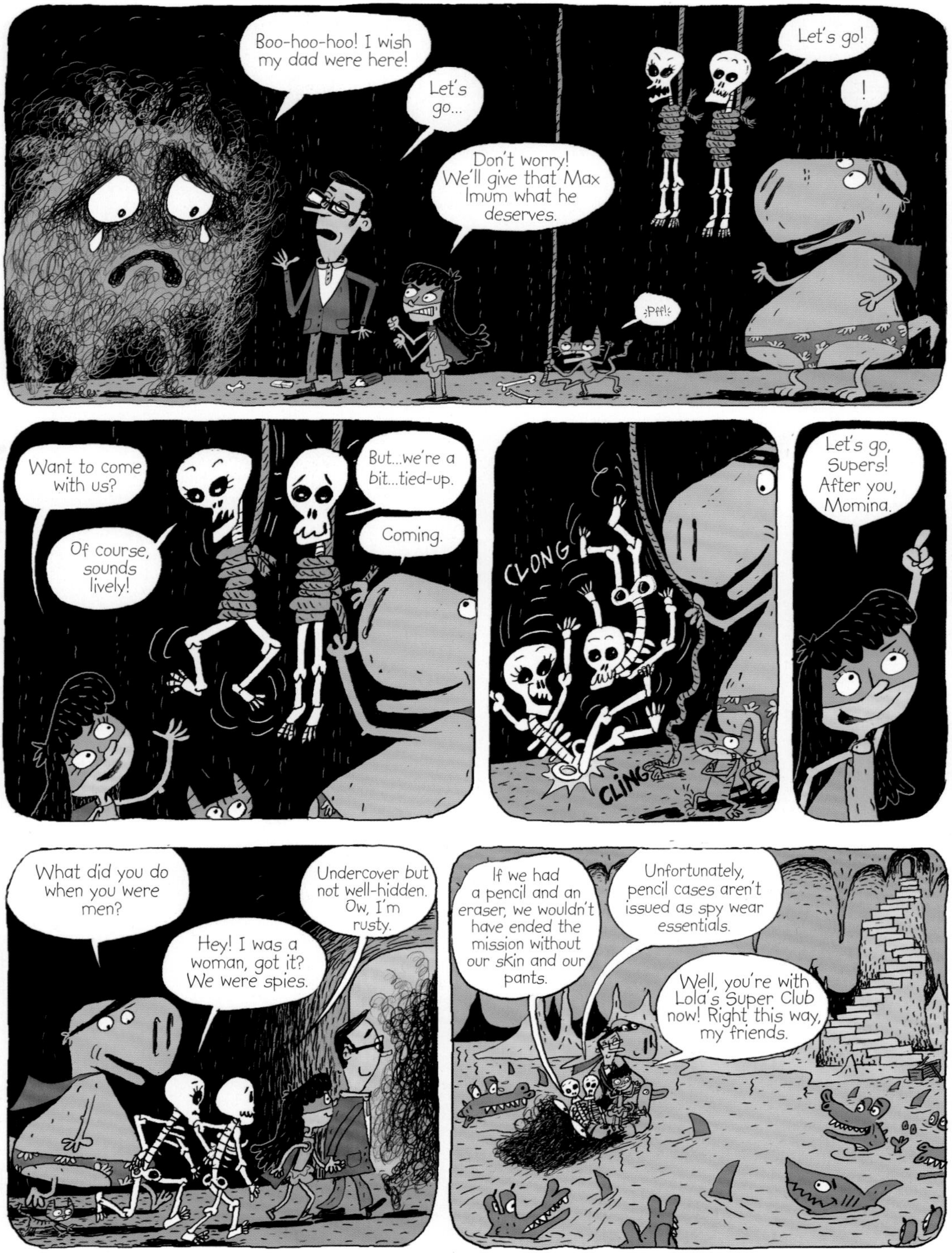

Boo-hoo-hoo! I wish my dad were here!
Let's go...
Don't worry! We'll give that Max Imum what he deserves.
Pff!
Let's go!
!
Want to come with us?
Of course, sounds lively!
But...we're a bit...tied-up.
Coming.
CLONG
CLING
Let's go, Supers! After you, Momina.
What did you do when you were men?
Hey! I was a woman, got it? We were spies.
Undercover but not well-hidden. Ow, I'm rusty.
If we had a pencil and an eraser, we wouldn't have ended the mission without our skin and our pants.
Unfortunately, pencil cases aren't issued as spy wear essentials.
Well, you're with Lola's Super Club now! Right this way, my friends.

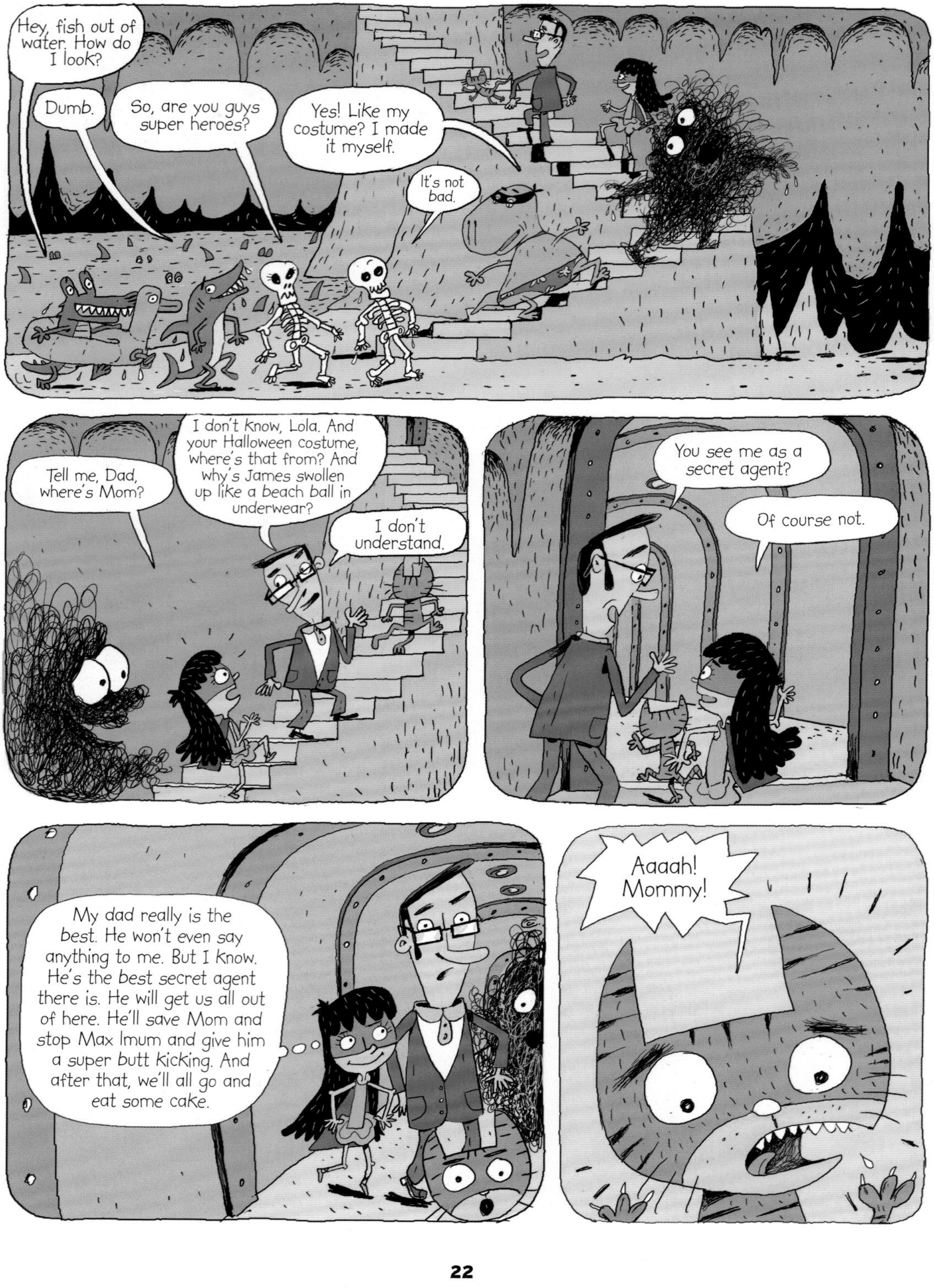
Hey, fish out of water. How do I look?
Dumb.
So, are you guys super heroes?
Yes! Like my costume? I made it myself.
It's not bad.
Tell me, Dad, where's Mom?
I don't know, Lola. And your Halloween costume, where's that from? And why's James swollen up like a beach ball in underwear?
I don't understand.
You see me as a secret agent?
Of course not.
My dad really is the best. He won't even say anything to me. But I know. He's the best secret agent there is. He will get us all out of here. He'll save Mom and stop Max Imum and give him a super butt kicking. And after that, we'll all go and eat some cake.
Aaaah! Mommy!

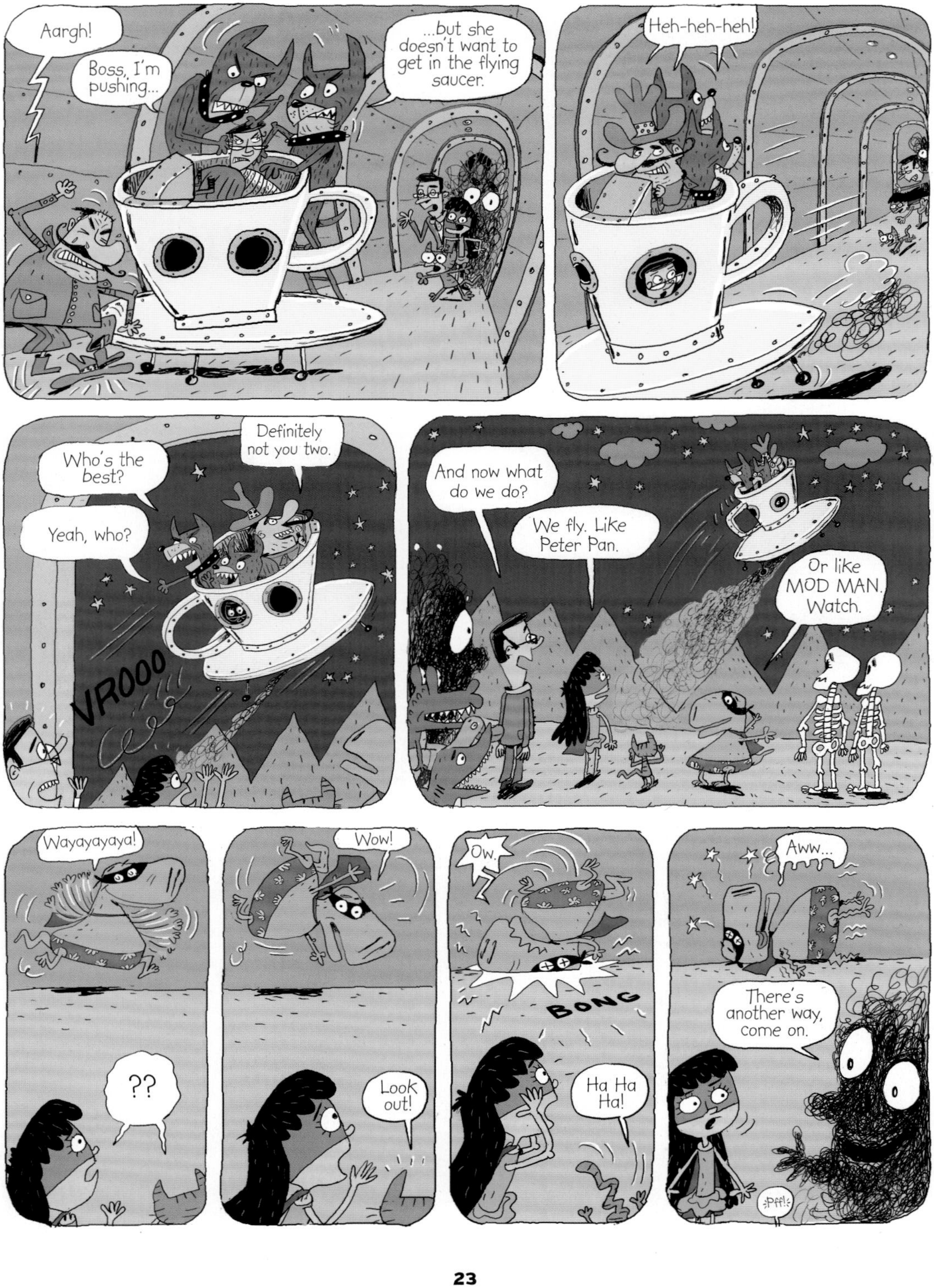
Aargh!
Boss, I'm pushing...
...but she doesn't want to get in the flying saucer.
Heh-heh-heh!
Who's the best?
Yeah, who?
Definitely not you two.
VROOO
And now what do we do?
We fly. Like Peter Pan.
Or like MOD MAN. Watch.
Wayayayaya!
??
Wow!
Look out!
Ow.
BONG
Ha Ha Ha!
Aww...
There's another way, come on.
Pff!

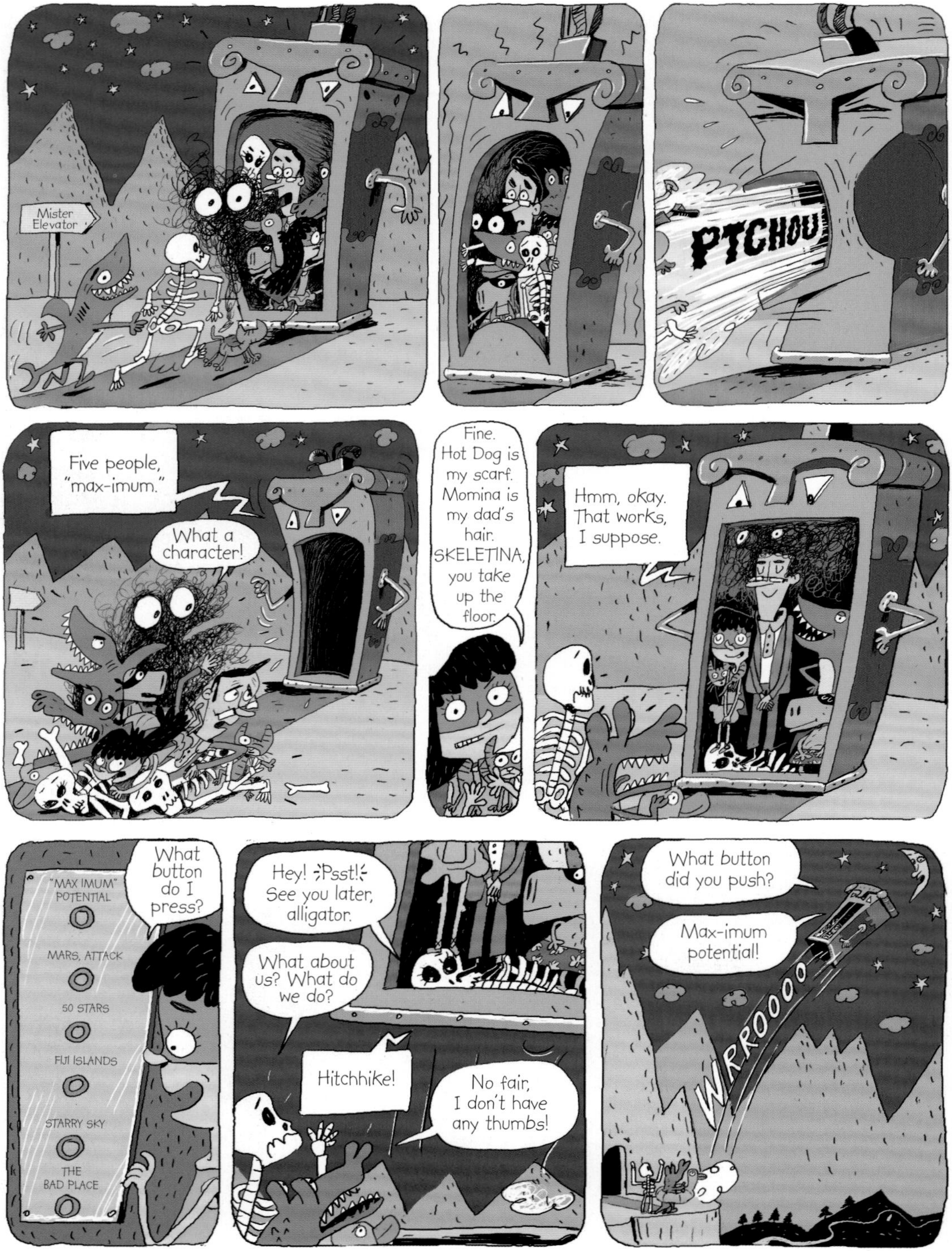
Mister Elevator
PTCHOU
Five people, "max-imum."
What a character!
Fine. Hot Dog is my scarf. Momina is my dad's hair. SKELETINA, you take up the floor.
Hmm, okay. That works, I suppose.
What button do I press?
"MAX IMUM" POTENTIAL
MARS, ATTACK
50 STARS
FIJI ISLANDS
STARRY SKY
THE BAD PLACE
Hey! Psst! See you later, alligator.
What about us? What do we do?
Hitchhike!
No fair, I don't have any thumbs!
What button did you push?
Max-imum potential!
WRROOOO

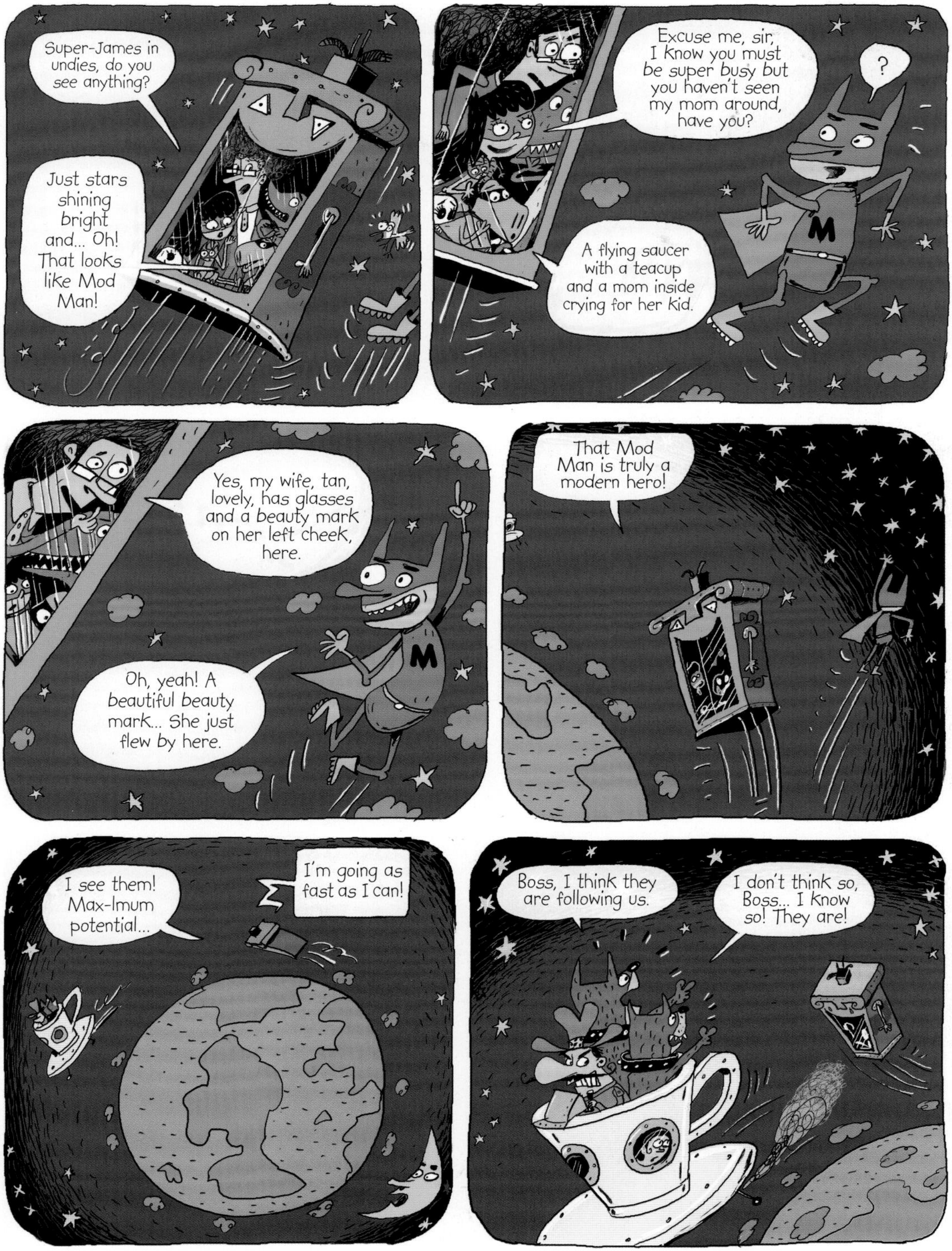

Super-James in undies, do you see anything?
Just stars shining bright and... Oh! That looks like Mod Man!
Excuse me, sir, I know you must be super busy but you haven't seen my mom around, have you?
?
A flying saucer with a teacup and a mom inside crying for her kid.
Yes, my wife, tan, lovely, has glasses and a beauty mark on her left cheek, here.
Oh, yeah! A beautiful beauty mark... She just flew by here.
That Mod Man is truly a modern hero!
I see them! Max-Imum potential...
I'm going as fast as I can!
Boss, I think they are following us.
I don't think so, Boss... I know so! They are!

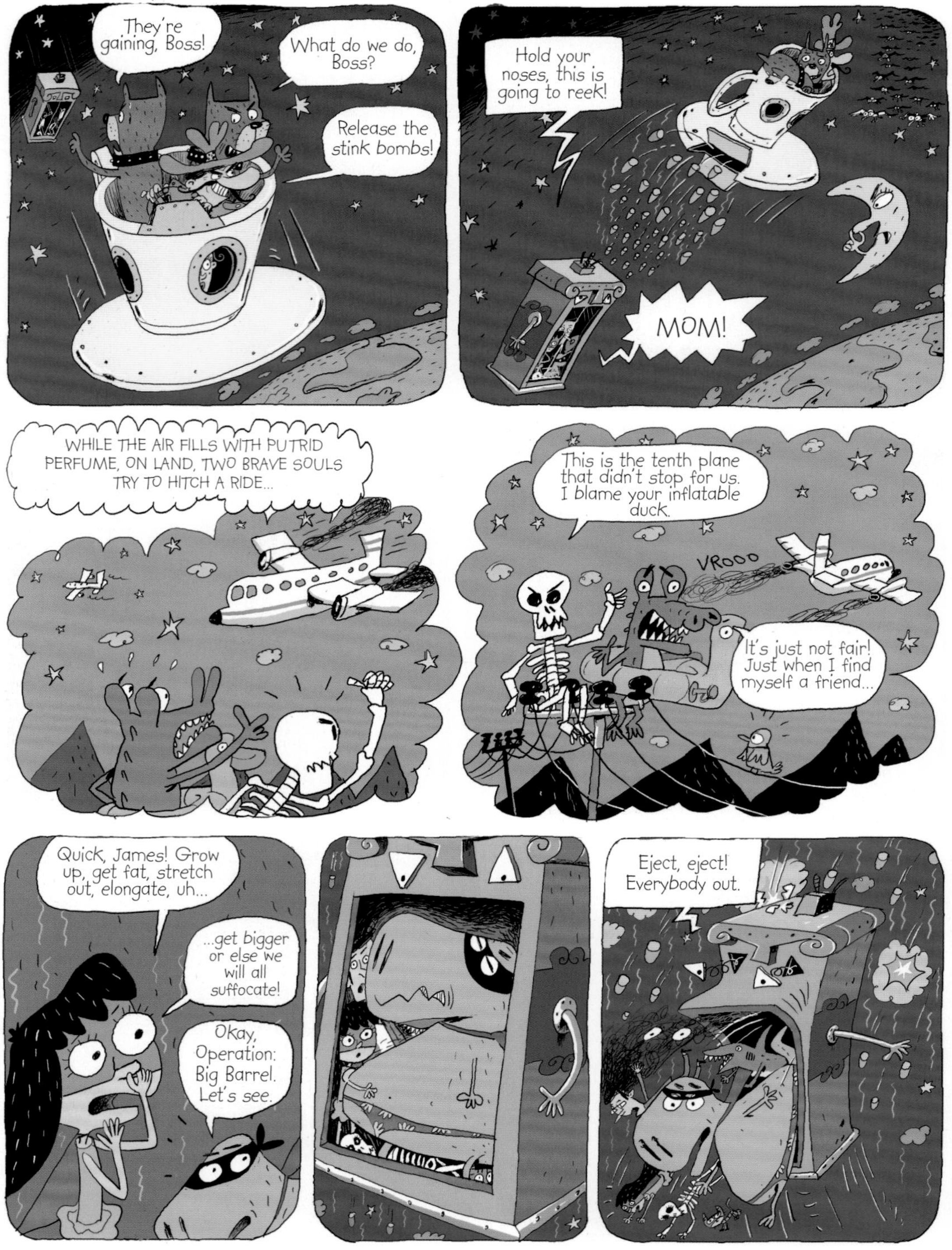

They're gaining, Boss!
What do we do, Boss?
Release the stink bombs!
Hold your noses, this is going to reek!
MOM!
WHILE THE AIR FILLS WITH PUTRID PERFUME, ON LAND, TWO BRAVE SOULS TRY TO HITCH A RIDE...
This is the tenth plane that didn't stop for us. I blame your inflatable duck.
VROOO
It's just not fair! Just when I find myself a friend...
Quick, James! Grow up, get fat, stretch out, elongate, uh...
...get bigger or else we will all suffocate!
Okay, Operation: Big Barrel. Let's see.
Eject, eject! Everybody out.

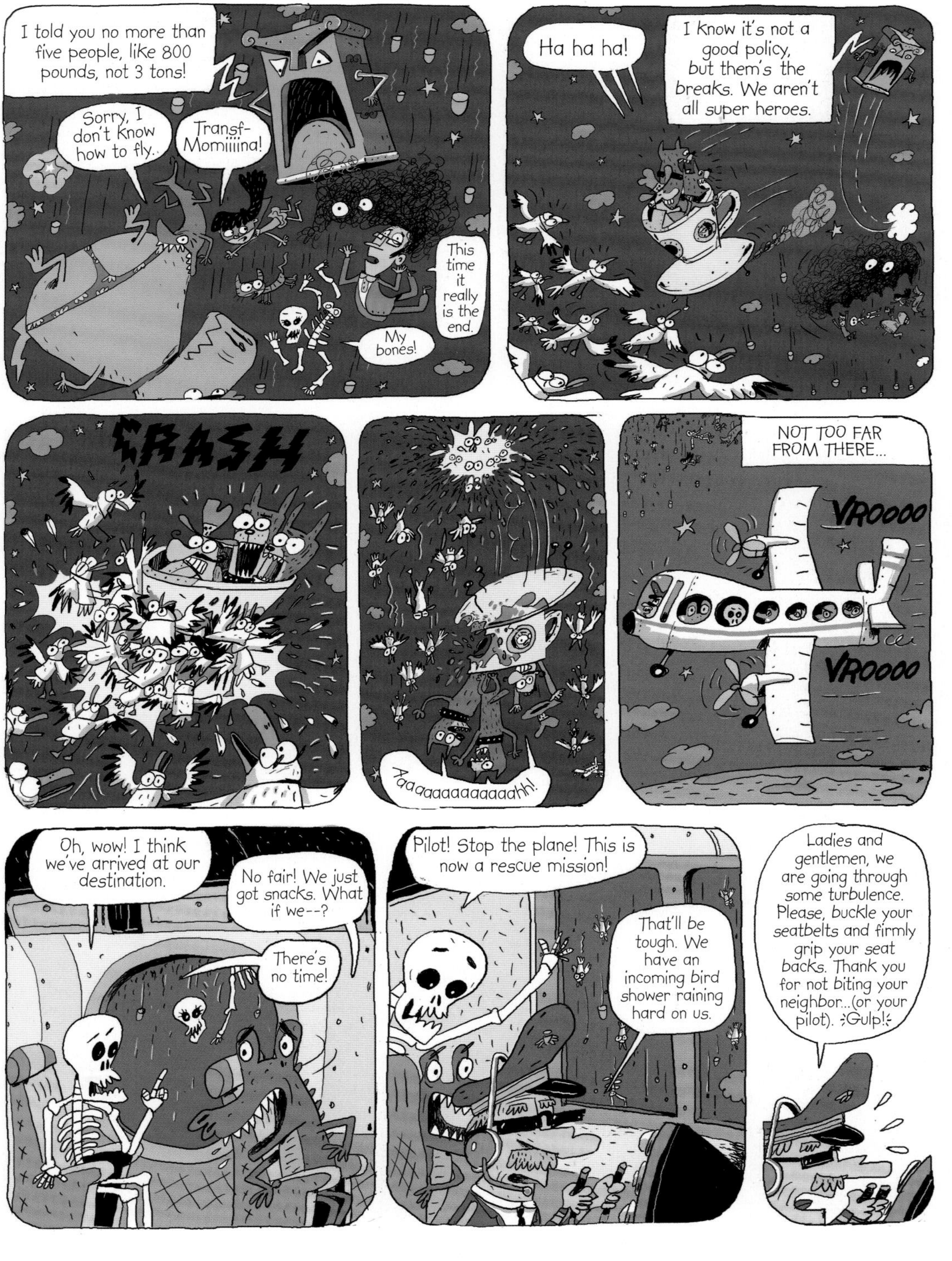
I told you no more than five people, like 800 pounds, not 3 tons!
Sorry, I don't Know how to fly.
Transf-Momiiiina!
This time it really is the end.
My bones!
Ha ha ha!
I Know it's not a good policy, but them's the breaks. We aren't all super heroes.
CRASH
Aaaaaaaaaaaaaahh!
NOT TOO FAR FROM THERE...
VROOOO
VROOOO
Oh, wow! I think we've arrived at our destination.
No fair! We just got snacks. What if we--?
There's no time!
Pilot! Stop the plane! This is now a rescue mission!
That'll be tough. We have an incoming bird shower raining hard on us.
Ladies and gentlemen, we are going through some turbulence. Please, buckle your seatbelts and firmly grip your seat backs. Thank you for not biting your neighbor...(or your pilot). Gulp!

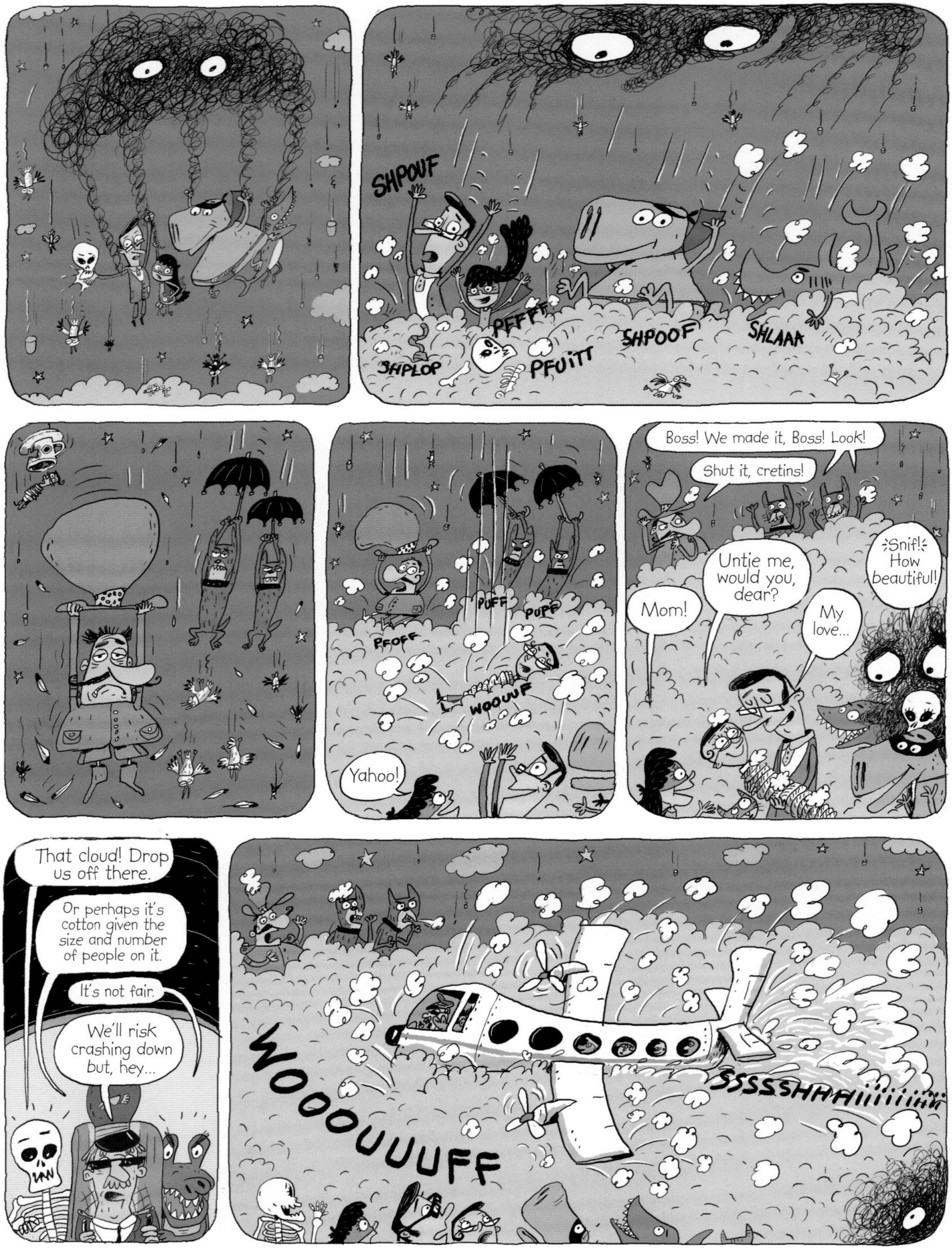
SHPOUF
PFFFF
SHPOOF
SHLAAA
SHPLOP
PFUITT
PUFF
PUFF
PFOFF
WOOUUF
Yahoo!
Boss! We made it, Boss! Look!
Shut it, cretins!
Untie me, would you, dear?
Mom!
My love...
Snif! How beautiful!
That cloud! Drop us off there.
Or perhaps it's cotton given the size and number of people on it.
It's not fair.
We'll risk crashing down but, hey...
WOOOUUUUFF
SSSSHHHiiiiiiiii

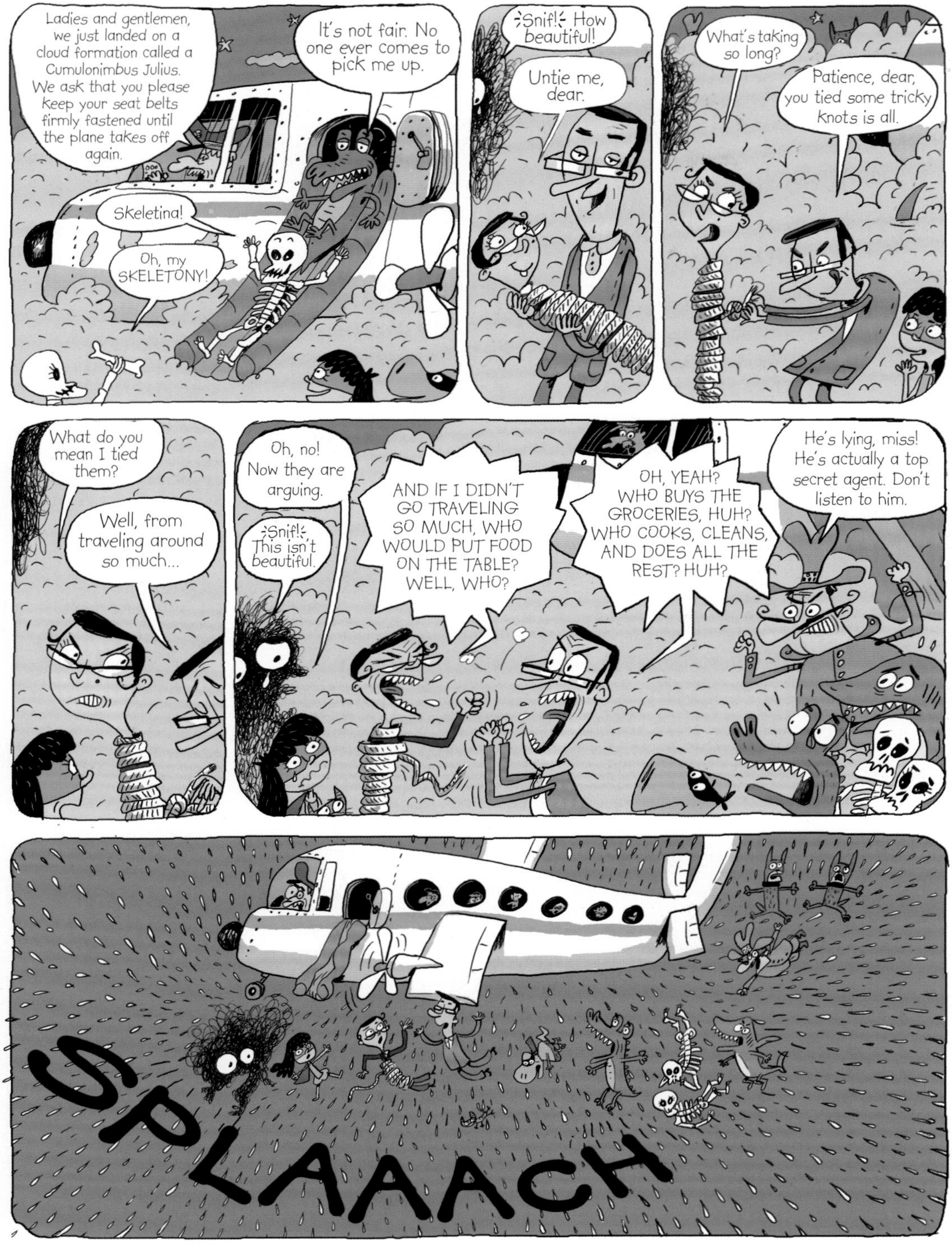
Ladies and gentlemen, we just landed on a cloud formation called a Cumulonimbus Julius. We ask that you please keep your seat belts firmly fastened until the plane takes off again.
It's not fair. No one ever comes to pick me up.
Skeletina!
Oh, my SKELETONY!
Snif! How beautiful!
Untie me, dear.
What's taking so long?
Patience, dear, you tied some tricky knots is all.
What do you mean I tied them?
Well, from traveling around so much...
Oh, no! Now they are arguing.
Snif! This isn't beautiful.
AND IF I DIDN'T GO TRAVELING SO MUCH, WHO WOULD PUT FOOD ON THE TABLE? WELL, WHO?
OH, YEAH? WHO BUYS THE GROCERIES, HUH? WHO COOKS, CLEANS, AND DOES ALL THE REST? HUH?
He's lying, miss! He's actually a top secret agent. Don't listen to him.
SPLAAACH

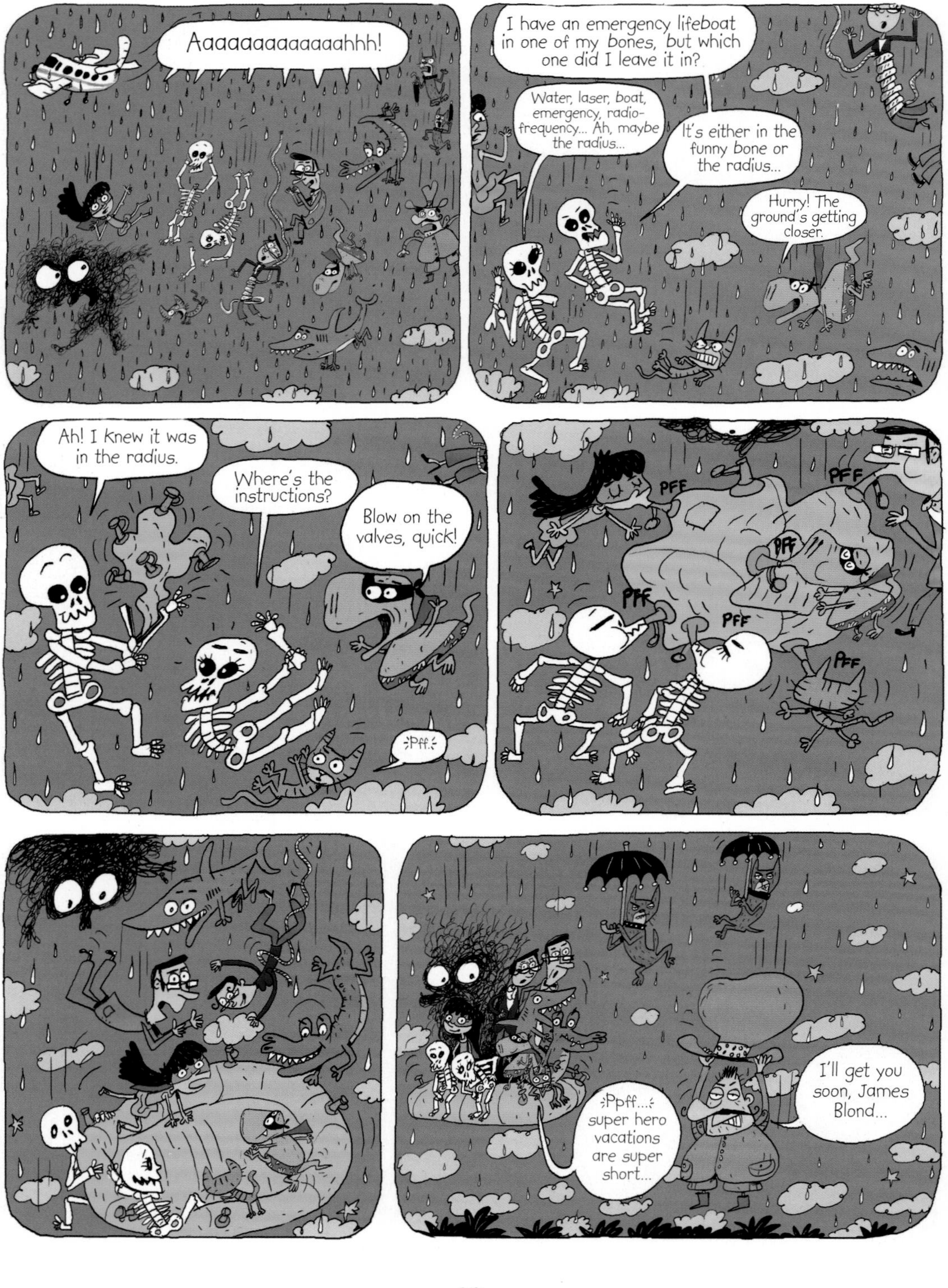
Aaaaaaaaaaaaahhh!
I have an emergency lifeboat in one of my bones, but which one did I leave it in?
Water, laser, boat, emergency, radio-frequency... Ah, maybe the radius...
It's either in the funny bone or the radius...
Hurry! The ground's getting closer.
Ah! I knew it was in the radius.
Where's the instructions?
Blow on the valves, quick!
Pff.
PFF
PFF
PFF
PFF
PFF
PFF
Ppff... super hero vacations are super short...
I'll get you soon, James Blond...

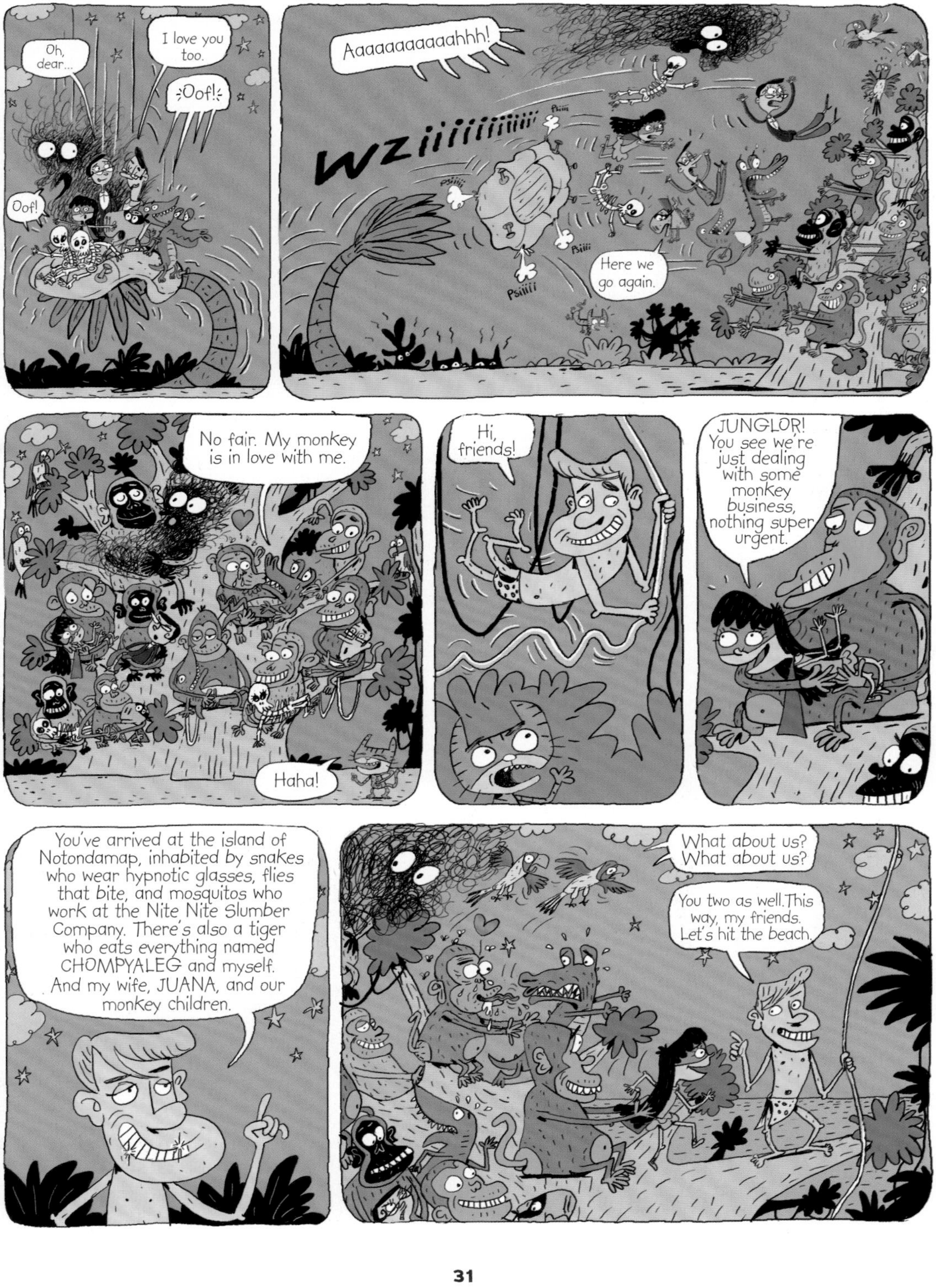

Oh, dear...
I love you too.
Oof!
Oof!
Aaaaaaaaaaahhh!
WZiiiiiiiiiii
Psiiii
Psiiii
Psiiii
Psiiiii
Here we go again.
No fair. My monkey is in love with me.
Haha!
Hi, friends!
JUNGLOR! You see we're just dealing with some monkey business, nothing super urgent.
You've arrived at the island of Notondamap, inhabited by snakes who wear hypnotic glasses, flies that bite, and mosquitos who work at the Nite Nite Slumber Company. There's also a tiger who eats everything named CHOMPYALEG and myself. And my wife, JUANA, and our monkey children.
What about us? What about us?
You two as well. This way, my friends. Let's hit the beach.

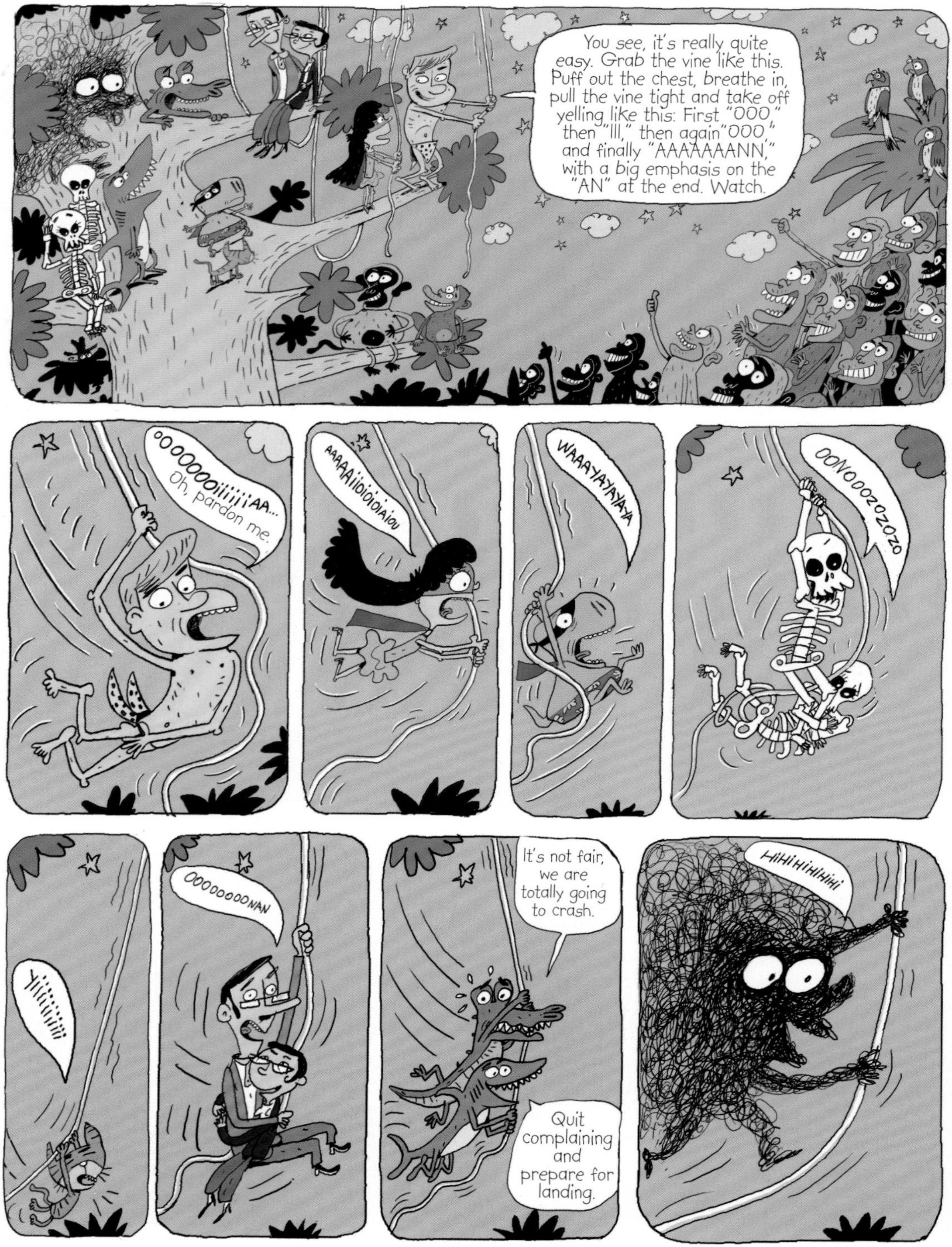
You see, it's really quite easy. Grab the vine like this. Puff out the chest, breathe in, pull the vine tight and take off yelling like this: First "OOO," then "III," then again "OOO," and finally "AAAAAAANN," with a big emphasis on the "AN" at the end. Watch.
OOOOOOiiiiiiAA... Oh, pardon me.
AAAAAAiioioioiAiou
WAAAYAYAYAYAYA
OONOOOZOZOZOZO
YIIIIiiiiiii
OOOOOOOONAN
It's not fair, we are totally going to crash.
Quit complaining and prepare for landing.
HIHIHIHIHIHIHI

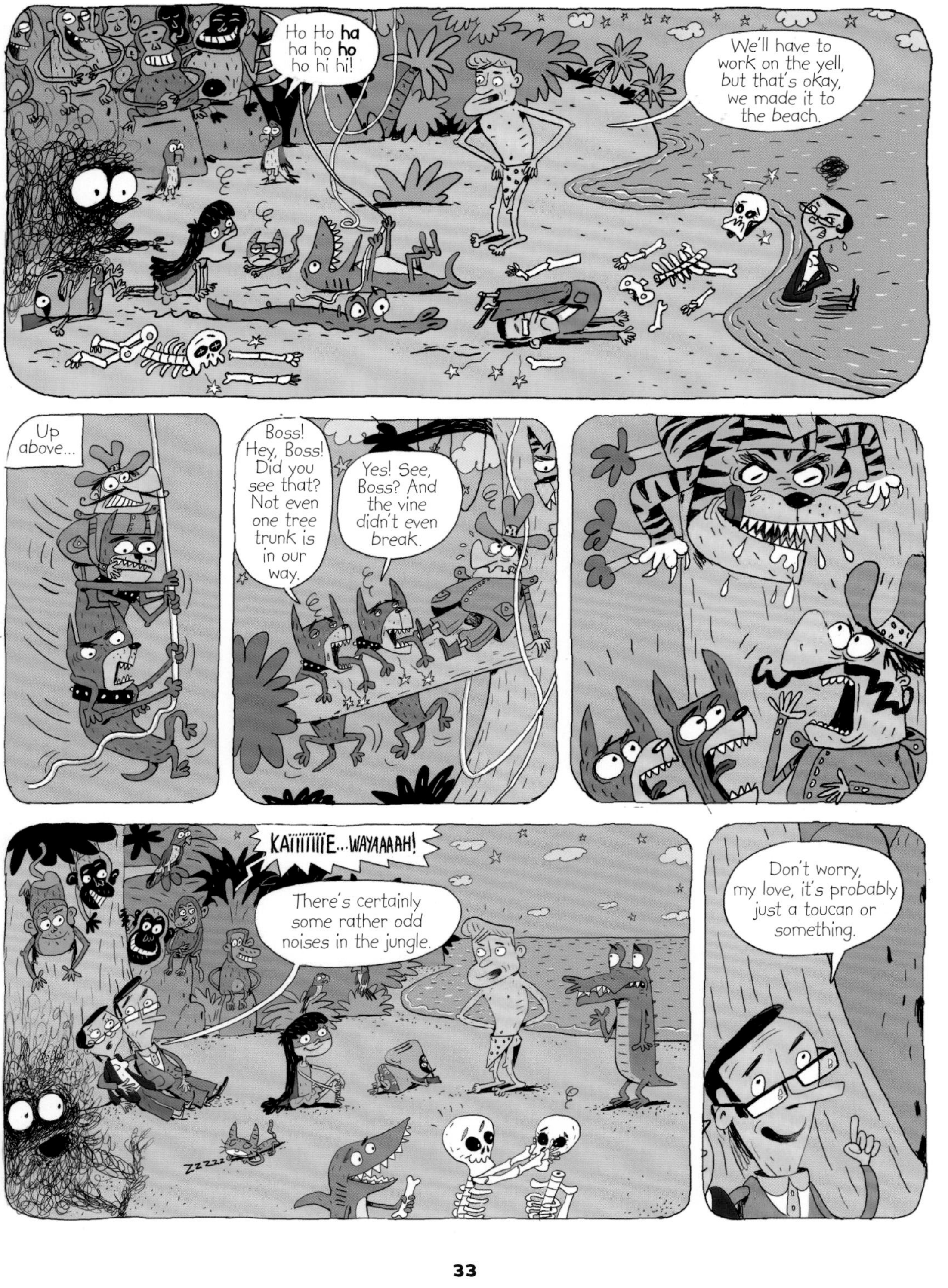
Ho Ho **ha** ha ho **ho** ho hi hi!
We'll have to work on the yell, but that's okay, we made it to the beach.
Up above...
Boss! Hey, Boss! Did you see that? Not even one tree trunk is in our way.
Yes! See, Boss? And the vine didn't even break.
KAÏÏÏÏÏÏE...WAYAAAAH!
There's certainly some rather odd noises in the jungle.
Zzzzz
Don't worry, my love, it's probably just a toucan or something.

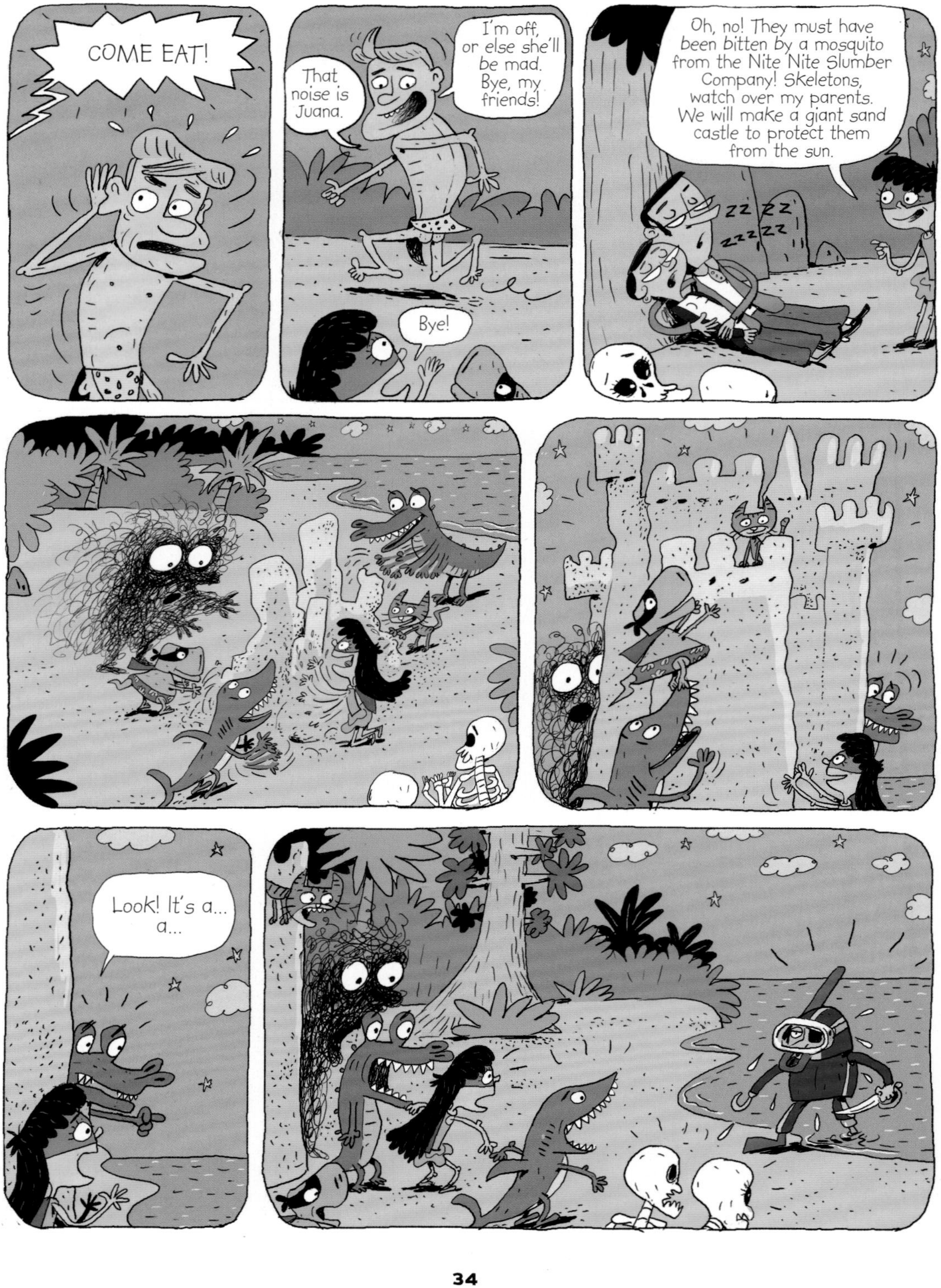
COME EAT!
That noise is Juana.
I'm off, or else she'll be mad. Bye, my friends!
Bye!
Oh, no! They must have been bitten by a mosquito from the Nite Nite Slumber Company! Skeletons, watch over my parents. We will make a giant sand castle to protect them from the sun.
ZZZ ZZ ZZZ ZZ
Look! It's a... a...

35

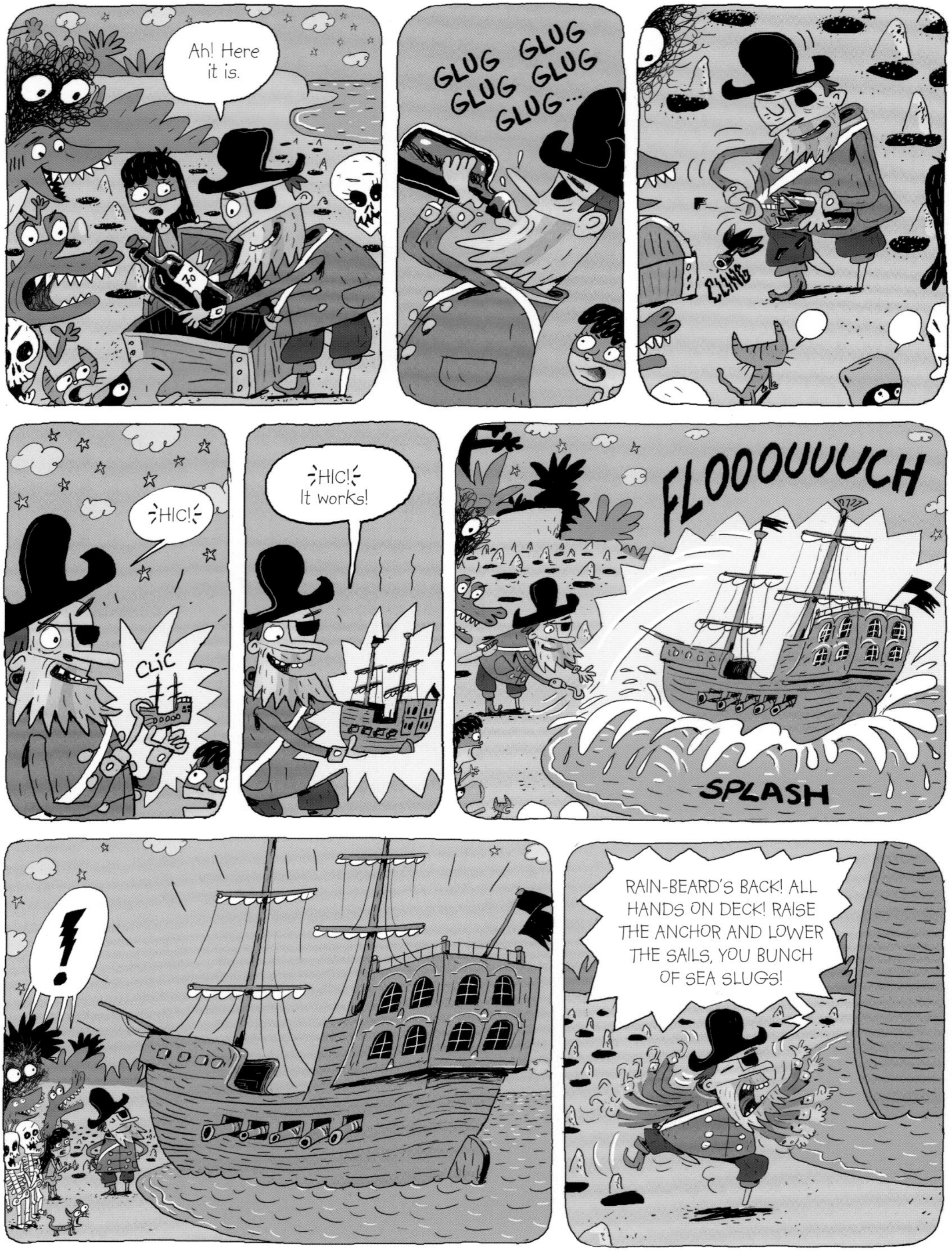
Ah! Here it is.
GLUG GLUG GLUG GLUG GLUG...
CLING
HIC!
CLIC
HIC! It works!
FLOOOUUUCH
SPLASH
!
RAIN-BEARD'S BACK! ALL HANDS ON DECK! RAISE THE ANCHOR AND LOWER THE SAILS, YOU BUNCH OF SEA SLUGS!

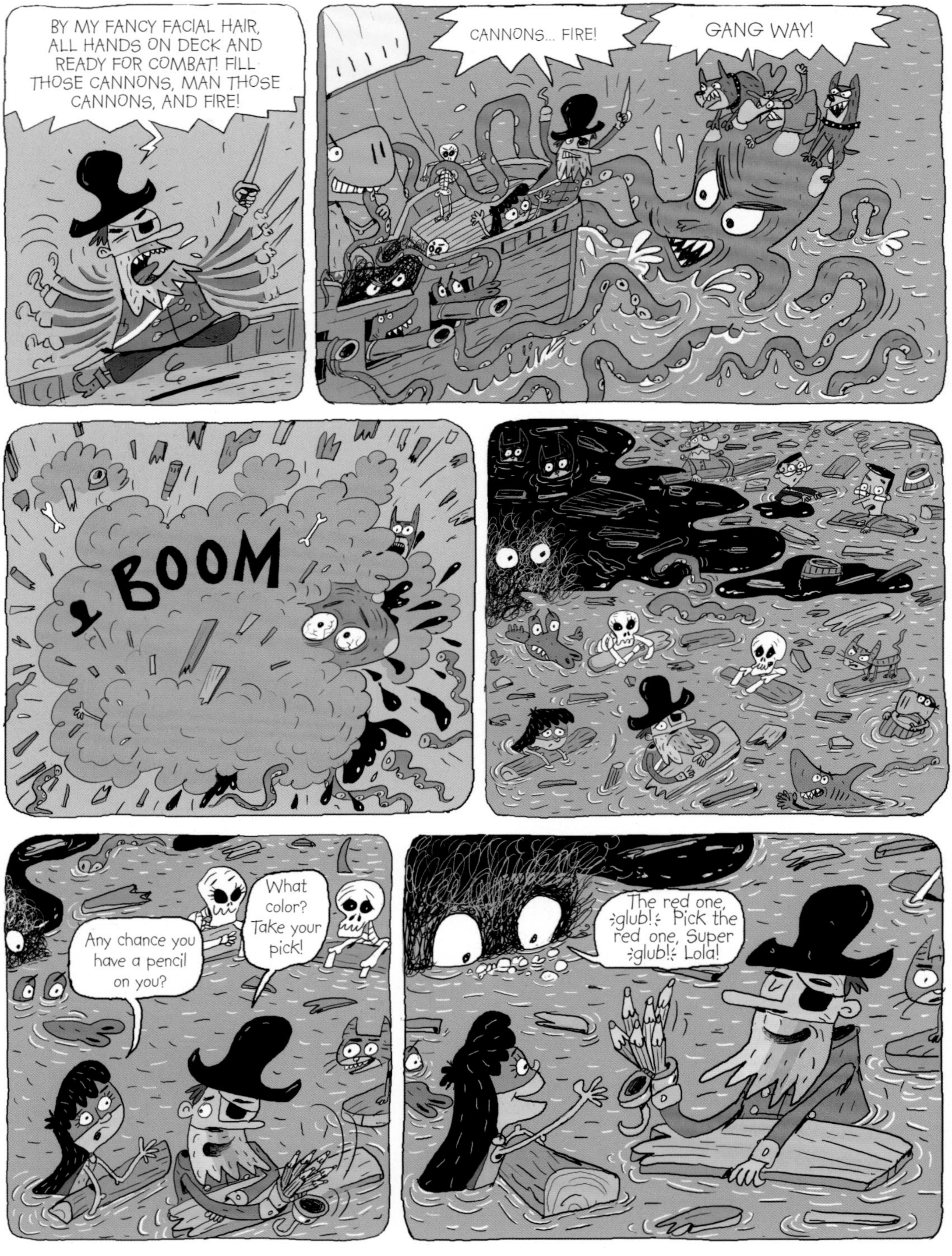
BY MY FANCY FACIAL HAIR, ALL HANDS ON DECK AND READY FOR COMBAT! FILL THOSE CANNONS, MAN THOSE CANNONS, AND FIRE!
CANNONS... FIRE!
GANG WAY!
BOOM
Any chance you have a pencil on you?
What color? Take your pick!
The red one, glub! Pick the red one, Super glub! Lola!

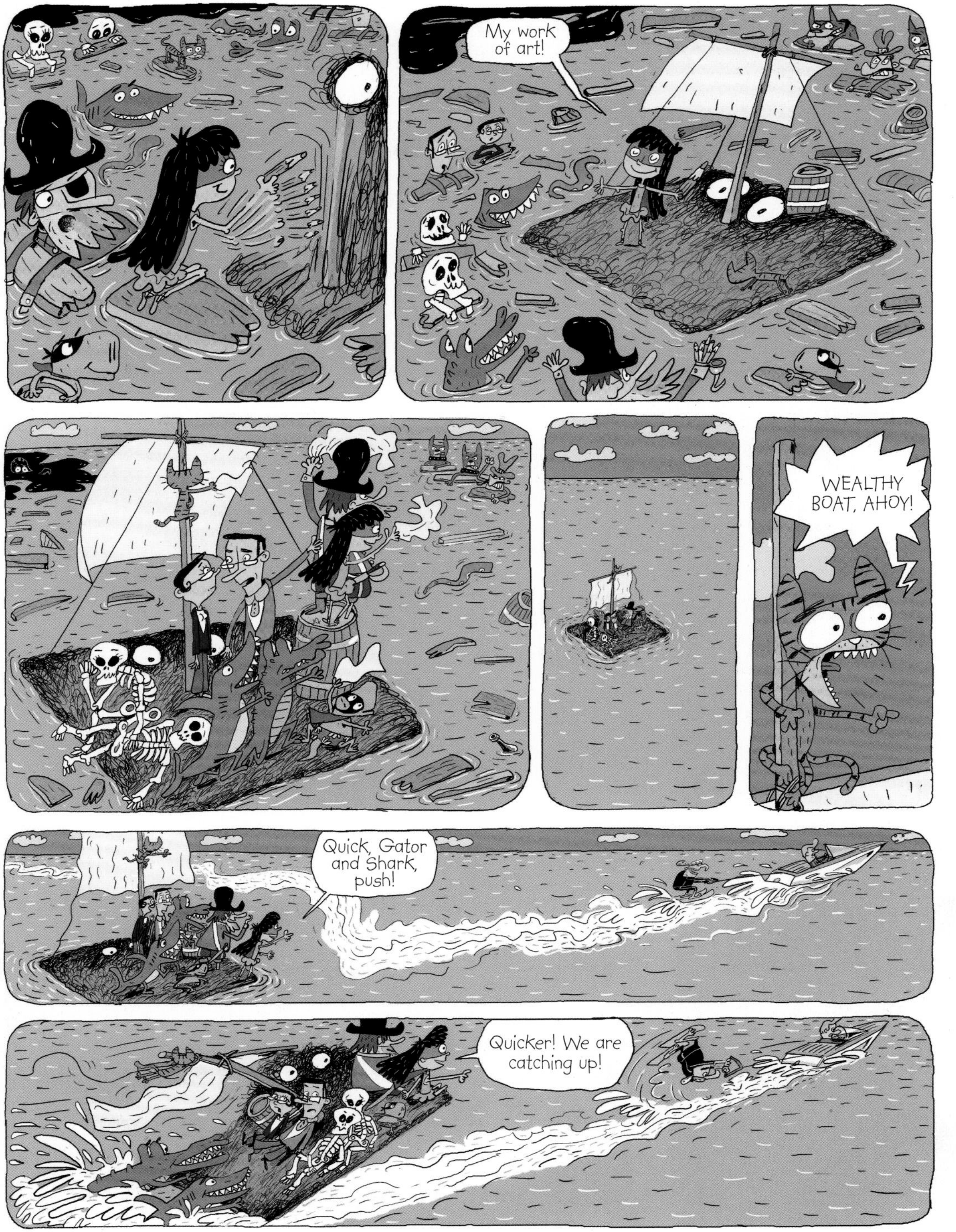
My work of art!
WEALTHY BOAT, AHOY!
Quick, Gator and Shark, push!
Quicker! We are catching up!

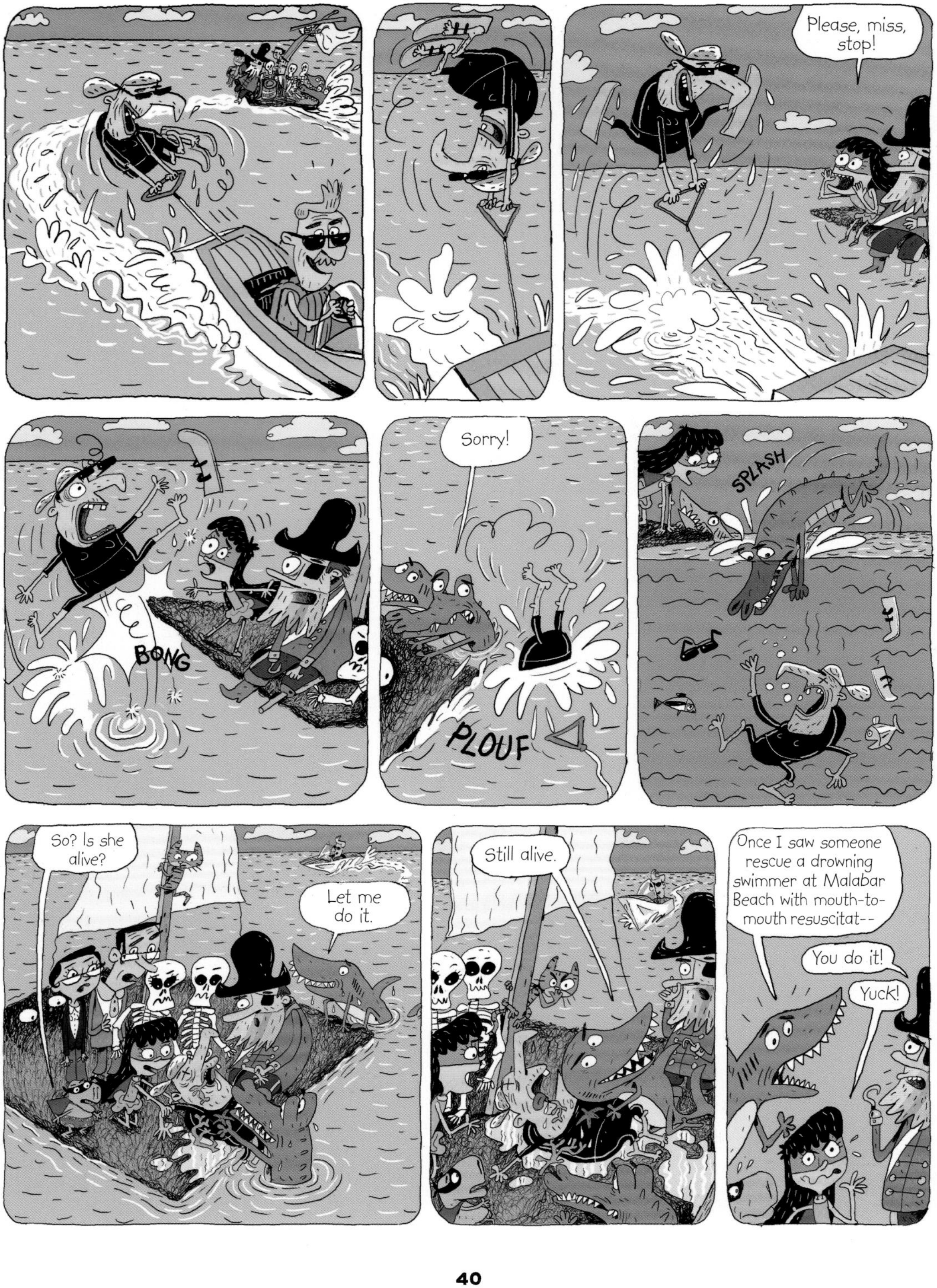
Please, miss, stop!
BONG
Sorry!
PLOUF
SPLASH
So? Is she alive?
Let me do it.
Still alive.
Once I saw someone rescue a drowning swimmer at Malabar Beach with mouth-to-mouth resuscitat--
You do it!
Yuck!

42

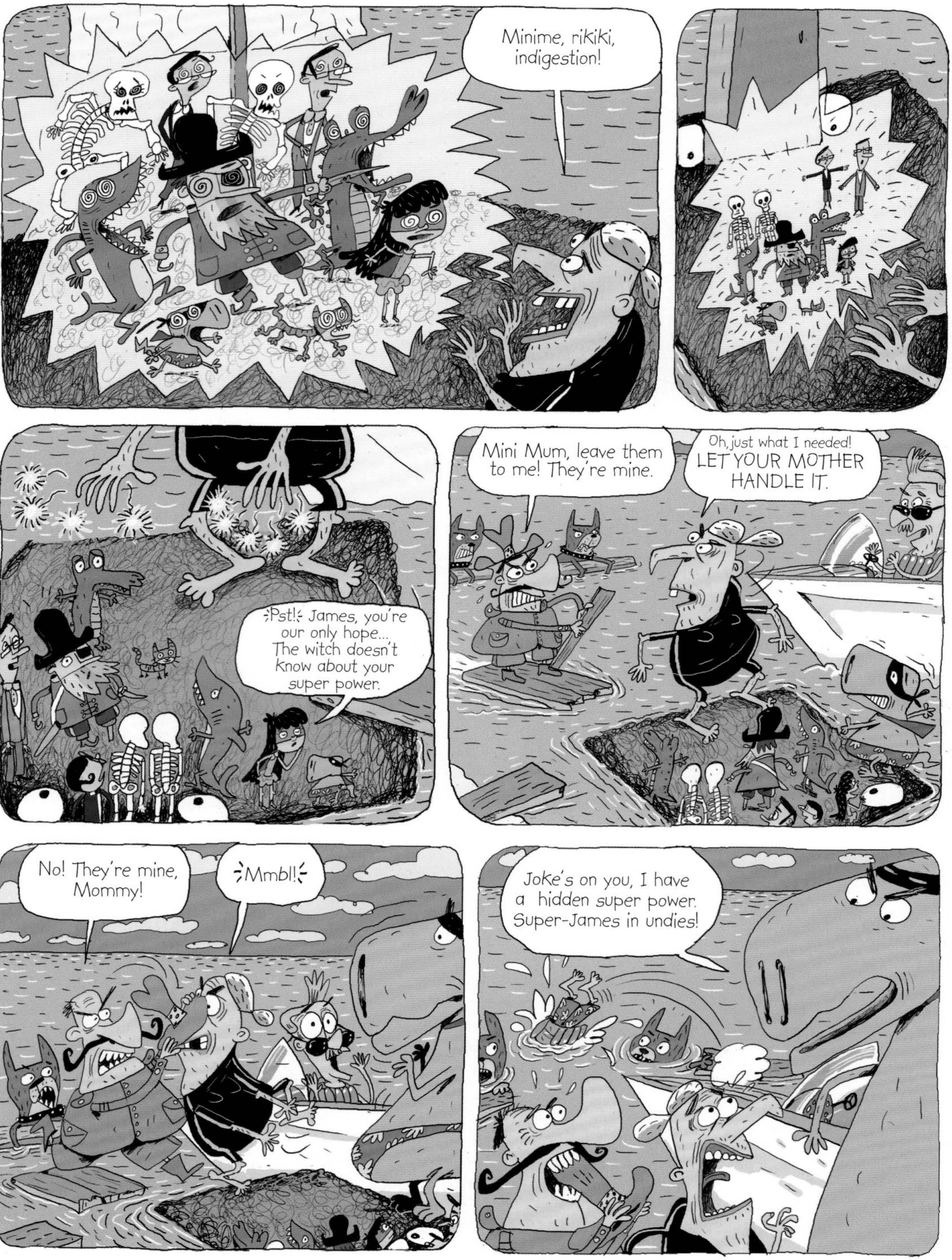
Minime, rikiki, indigestion!
Pst! James, you're our only hope... The witch doesn't know about your super power.
Mini Mum, leave them to me! They're mine.
Oh, just what I needed! LET YOUR MOTHER HANDLE IT.
No! They're mine, Mommy!
Mmbl!
Joke's on you, I have a hidden super power. Super-James in undies!

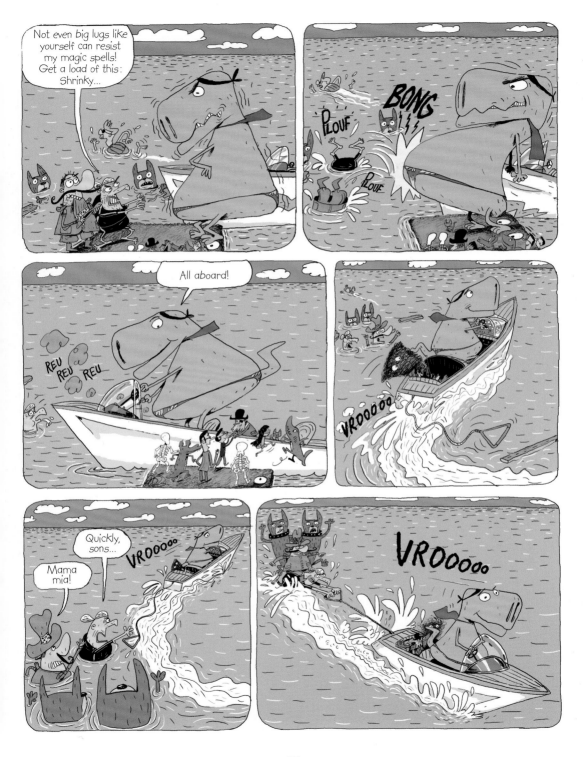

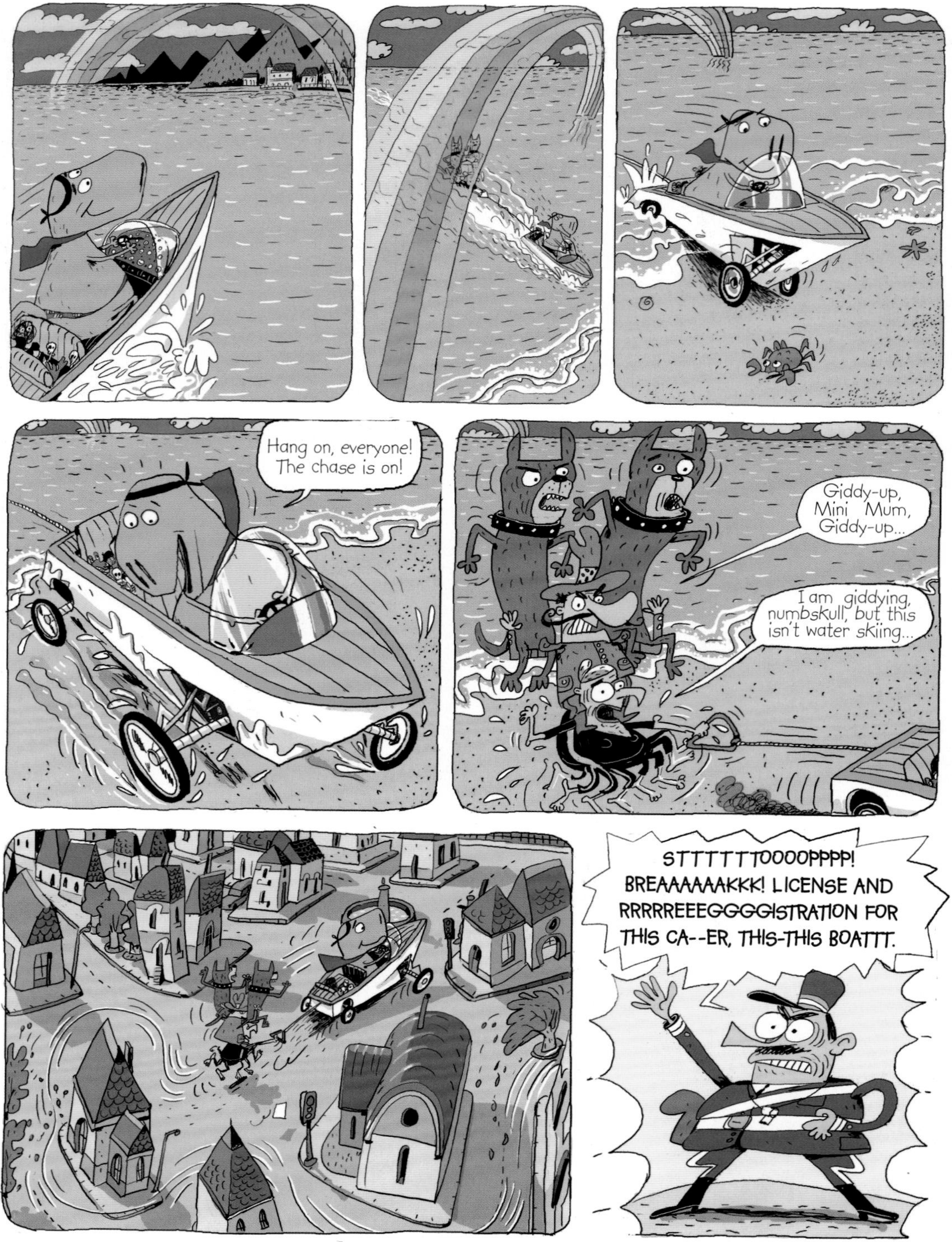
Hang on, everyone! The chase is on!
Giddy-up, Mini Mum, Giddy-up...
I am giddying, numbskull, but this isn't water skiing...
STTTTTTOOOOPPPP! BREAAAAAAKKK! LICENSE AND RRRRREEEGGGGISTRATION FOR THIS CA--ER, THIS-THIS BOATTT.

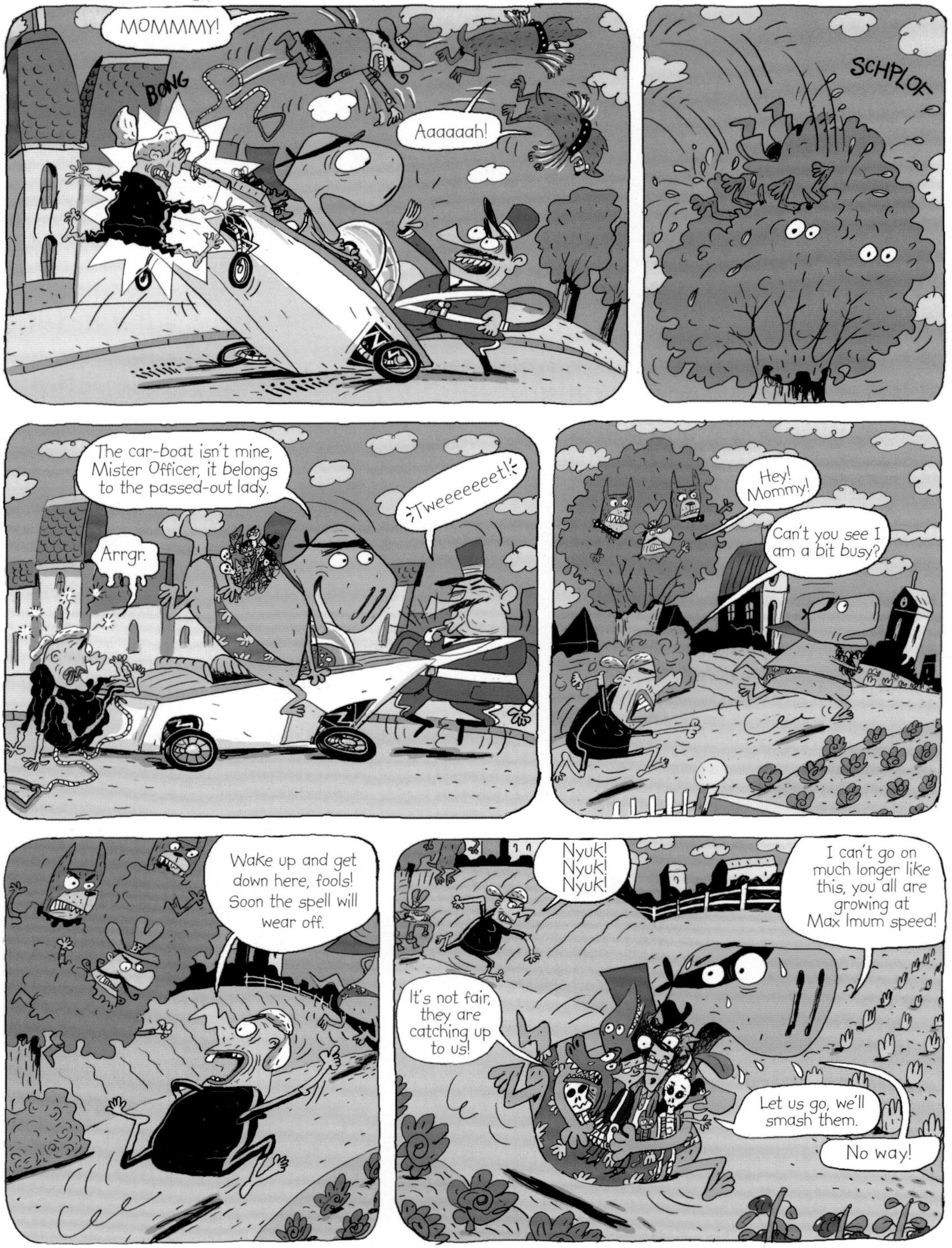
MOMMMY!
BONG
Aaaaaah!
SCHPLOF
The car-boat isn't mine, Mister Officer, it belongs to the passed-out lady.
Tweeeeeeet!
Arrgr.
Hey! Mommy!
Can't you see I am a bit busy?
Wake up and get down here, fools! Soon the spell will wear off.
Nyuk! Nyuk! Nyuk!
I can't go on much longer like this, you all are growing at Max Imum speed!
It's not fair, they are catching up to us!
Let us go, we'll smash them.
No way!

48

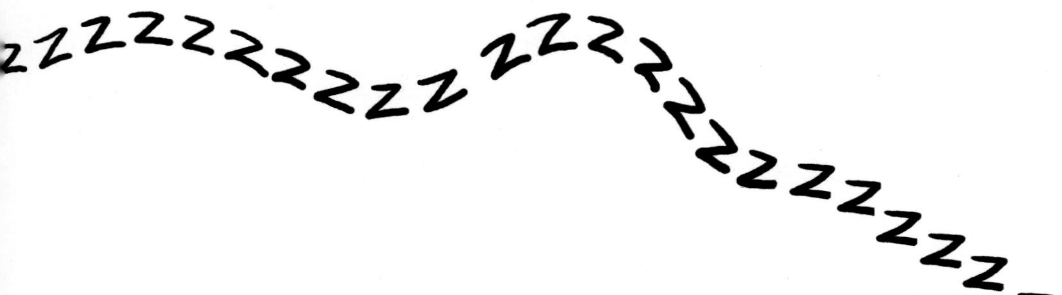
zZZZZZZZZZZZZZZZZZZZZZz

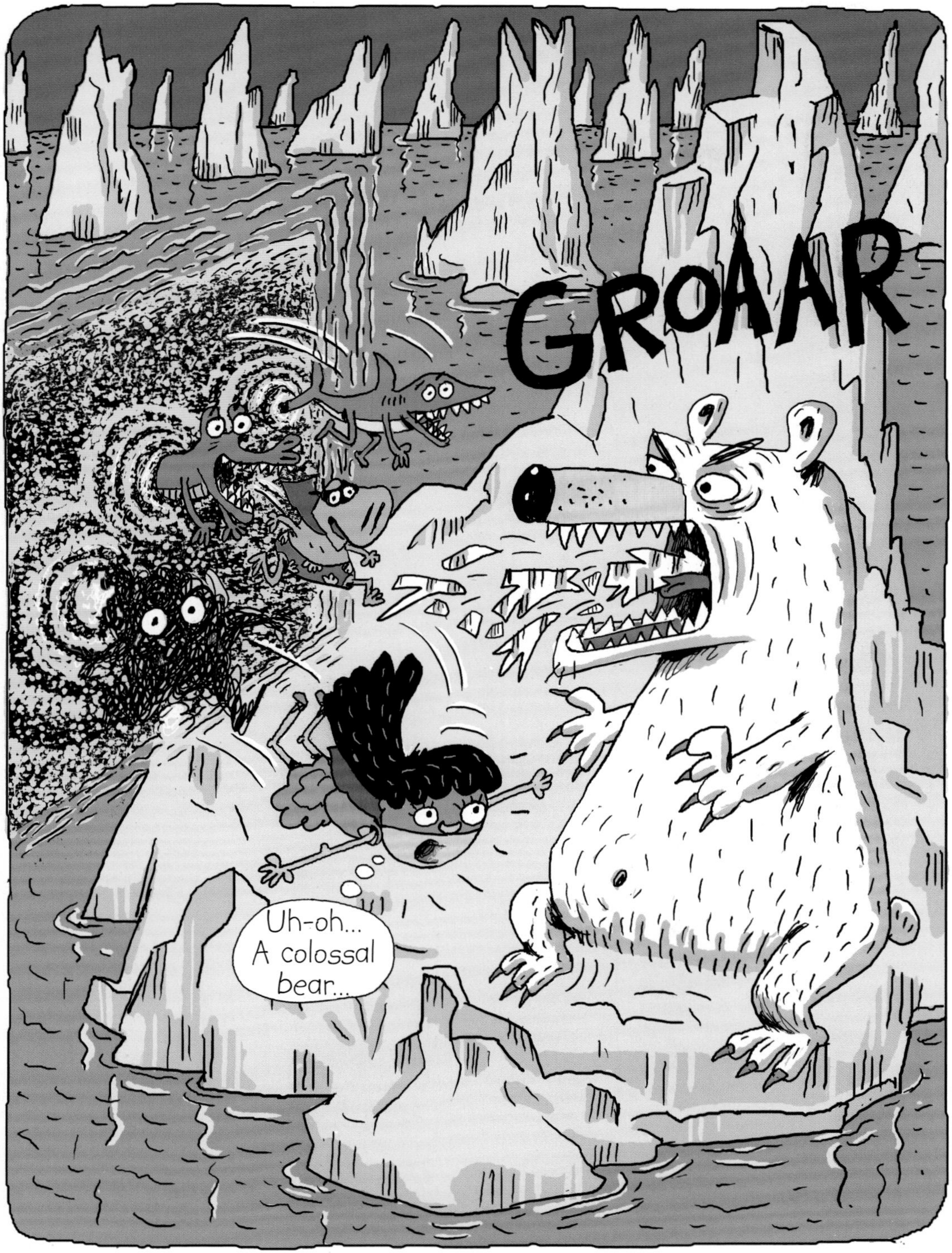
GROAAR
Uh-oh...
A colossal
bear...

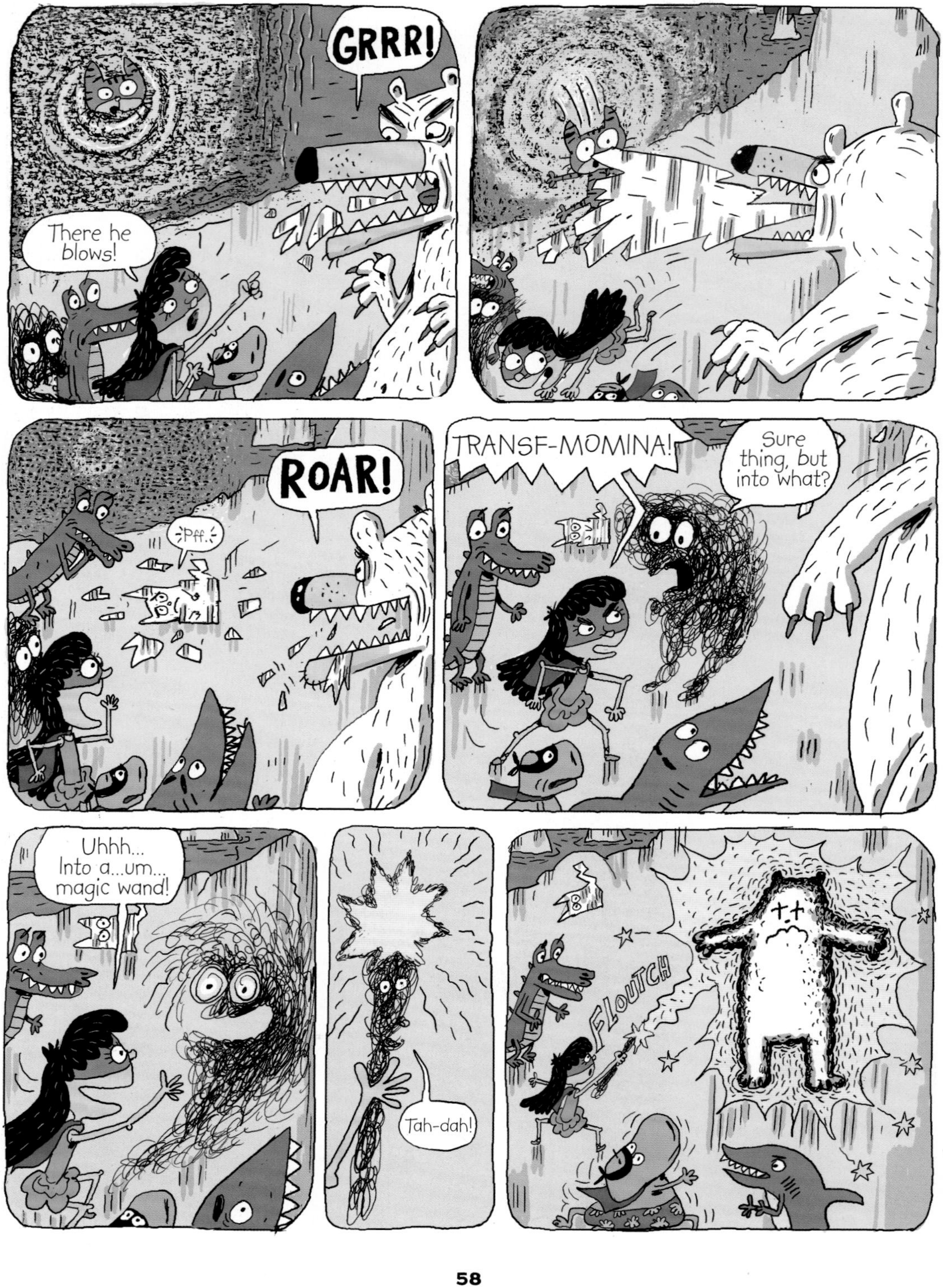
There he blows!
GRRR!
ROAR!
Pff..
TRANSF-MOMINA!
Sure thing, but into what?
Uhhh... Into a...um... magic wand!
Tah-dah!
FLOUTCH

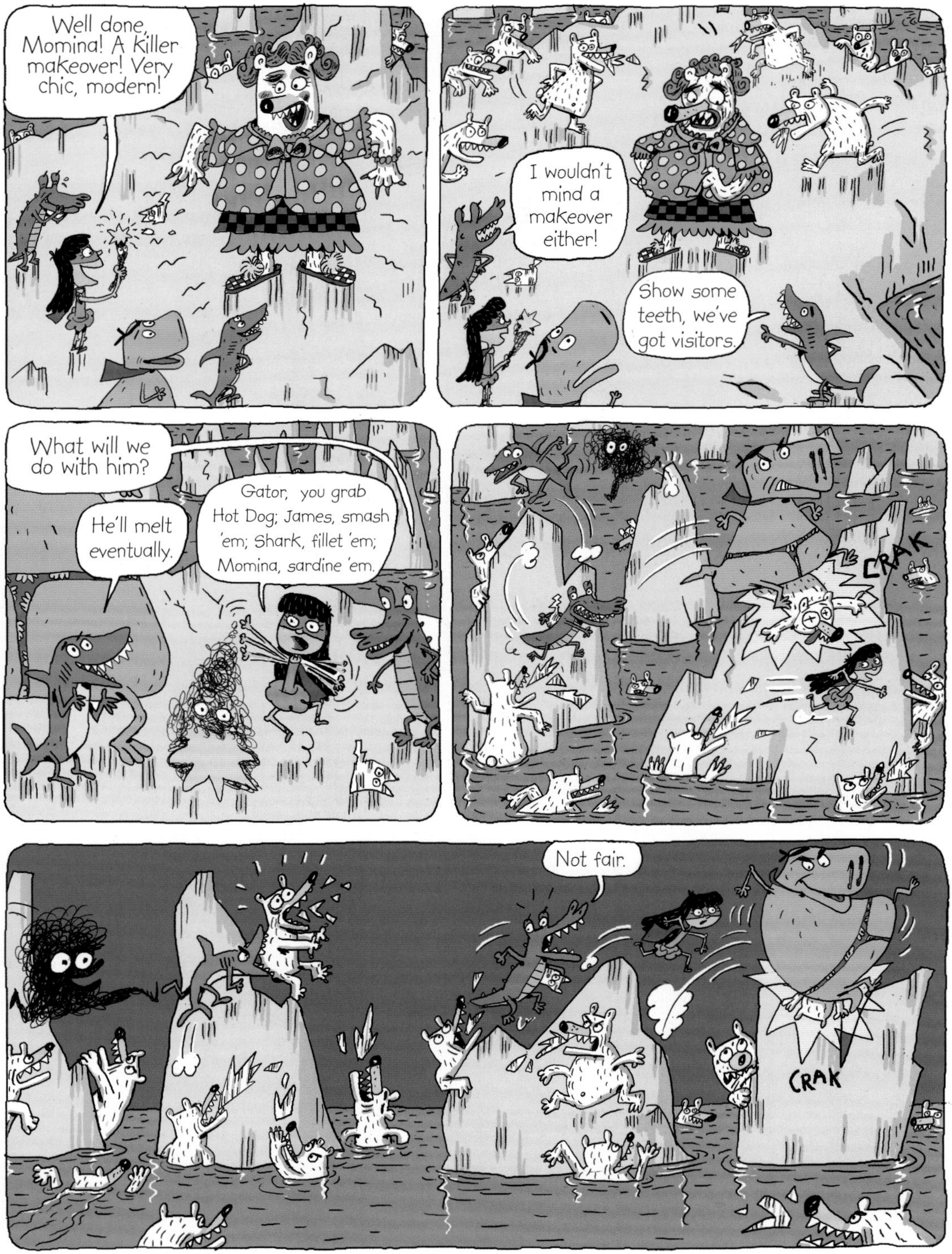
Well done, Momina! A killer makeover! Very chic, modern!
I wouldn't mind a makeover either!
Show some teeth, we've got visitors.
What will we do with him?
He'll melt eventually.
Gator, you grab Hot Dog; James, smash 'em; Shark, fillet 'em; Momina, sardine 'em.
CRAK
Not fair.
CRAK

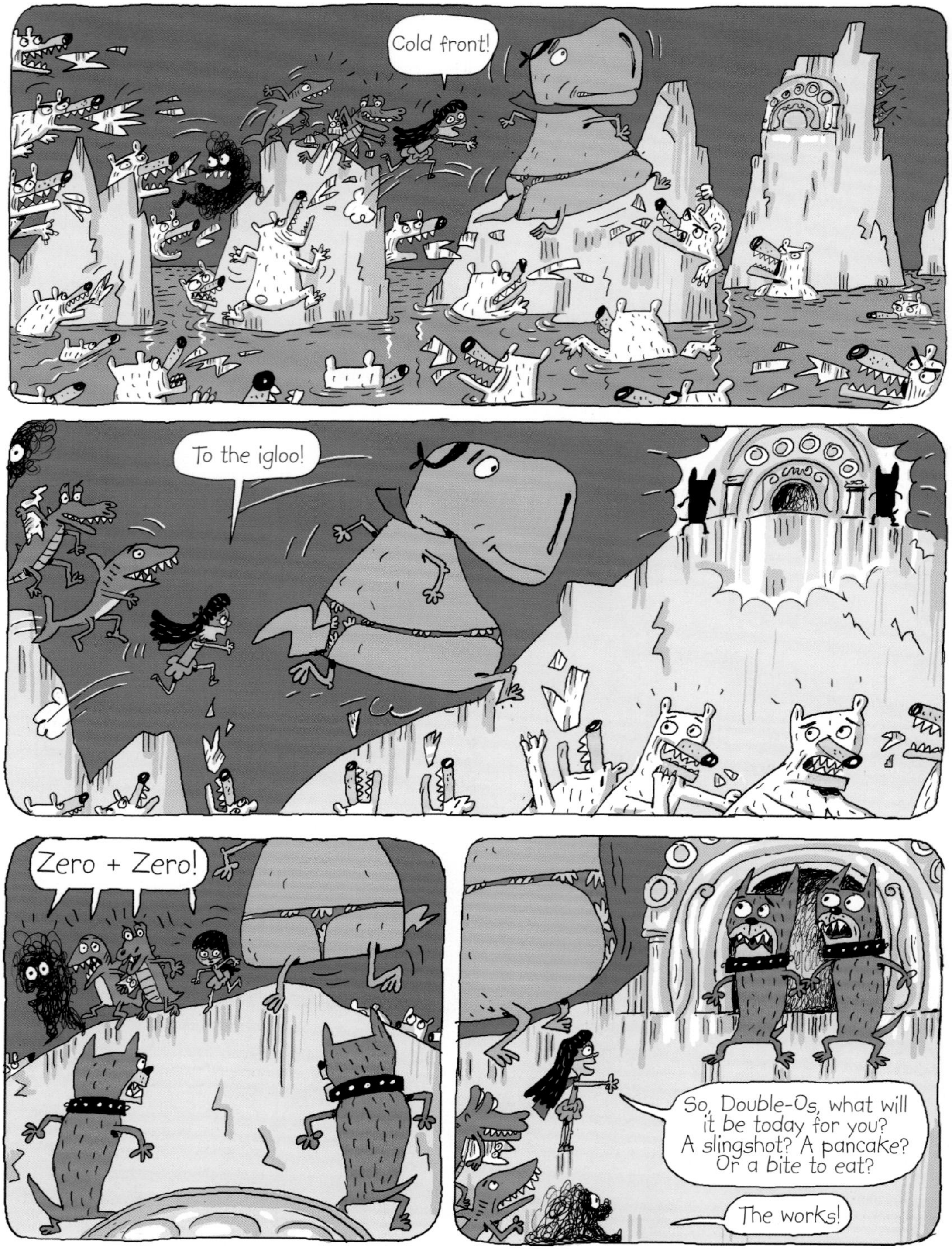
Cold front!
To the igloo!
Zero + Zero!
So, Double-Os, what will it be today for you? A slingshot? A pancake? Or a bite to eat?
The works!

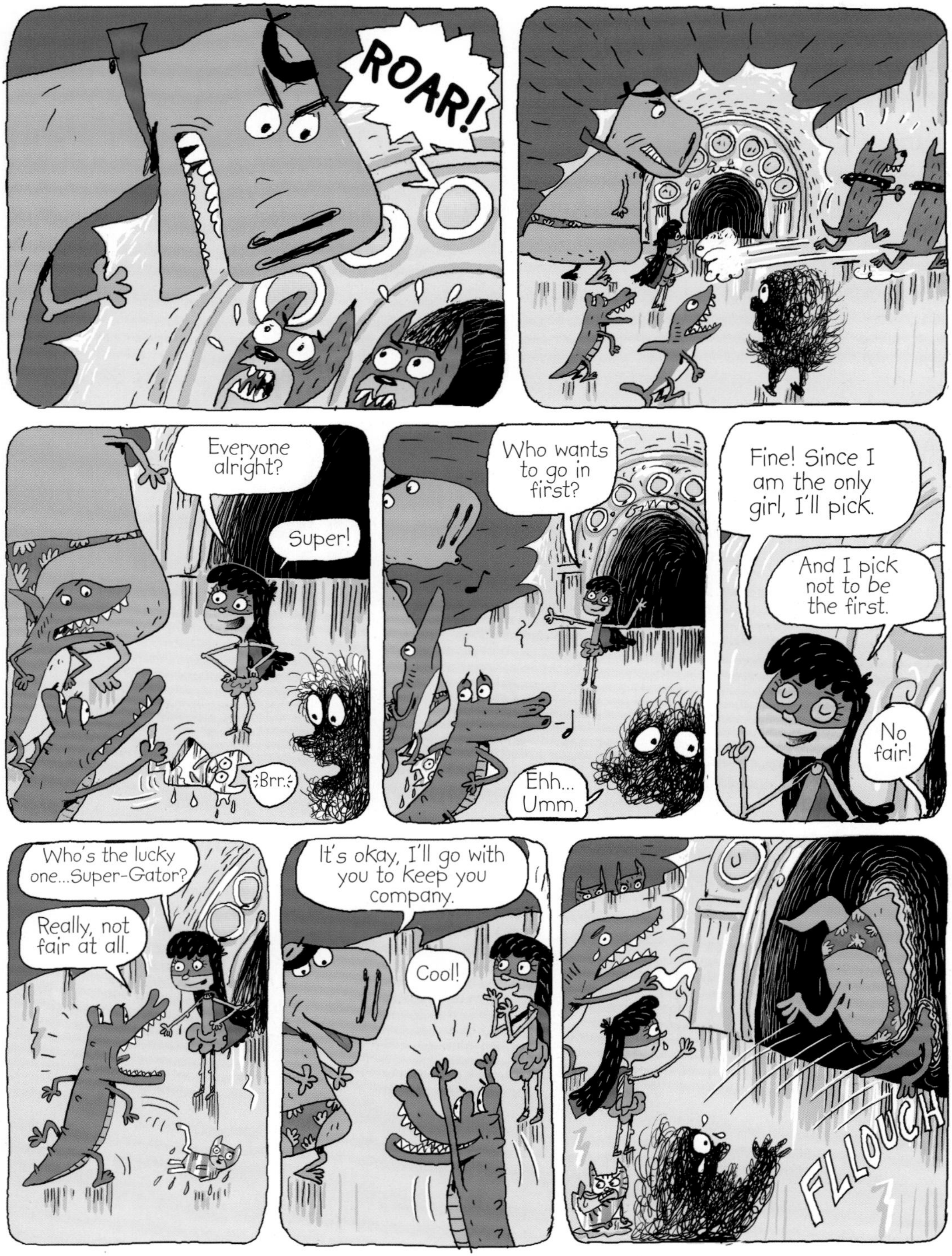
ROAR!
Everyone alright?
Super!
Brr.
Who wants to go in first?
Ehh... Umm.
Fine! Since I am the only girl, I'll pick.
And I pick not to be the first.
No fair!
Who's the lucky one...Super-Gator?
Really, not fair at all.
It's okay, I'll go with you to keep you company.
Cool!
FLLOUCH

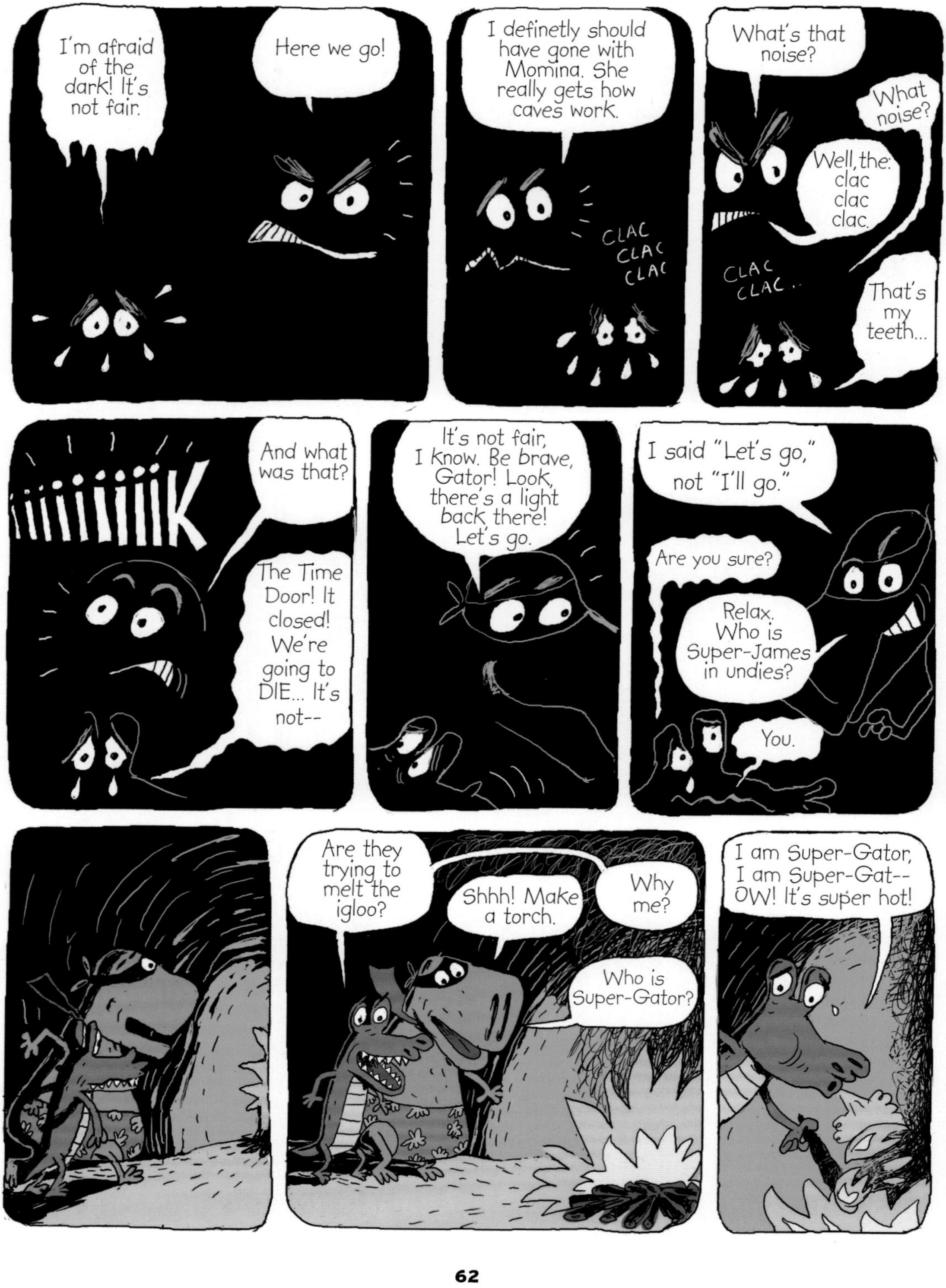
I'm afraid of the dark! It's not fair.
Here we go!
I definetly should have gone with Momina. She really gets how caves work.
CLAC CLAC CLAC
What's that noise?
What noise?
Well, the: clac clac clac.
CLAC CLAC...
That's my teeth...
iiiiiiiiiiK
And what was that?
The Time Door! It closed! We're going to DIE... It's not--
It's not fair, I know. Be brave, Gator! Look, there's a light back there! Let's go.
I said "Let's go," not "I'll go."
Are you sure?
Relax. Who is Super-James in undies?
You.
Are they trying to melt the igloo?
Shhh! Make a torch.
Why me?
Who is Super-Gator?
I am Super-Gator, I am Super-Gat-- OW! It's super hot!

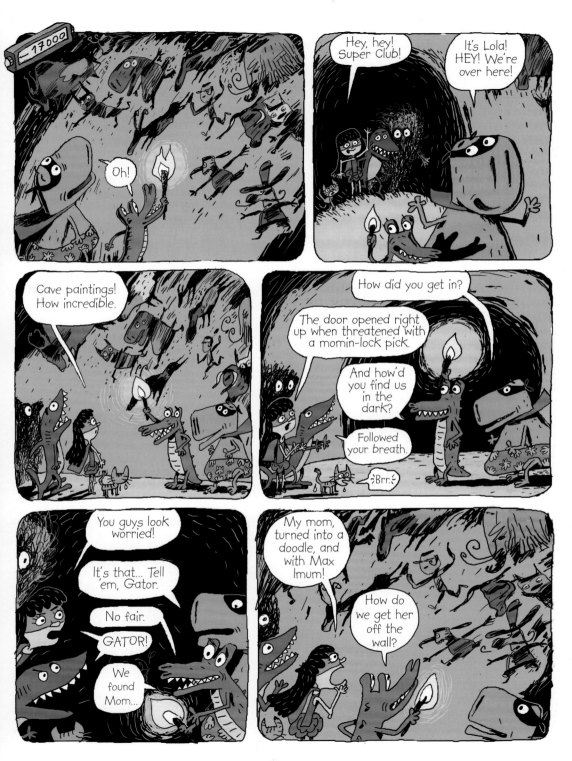

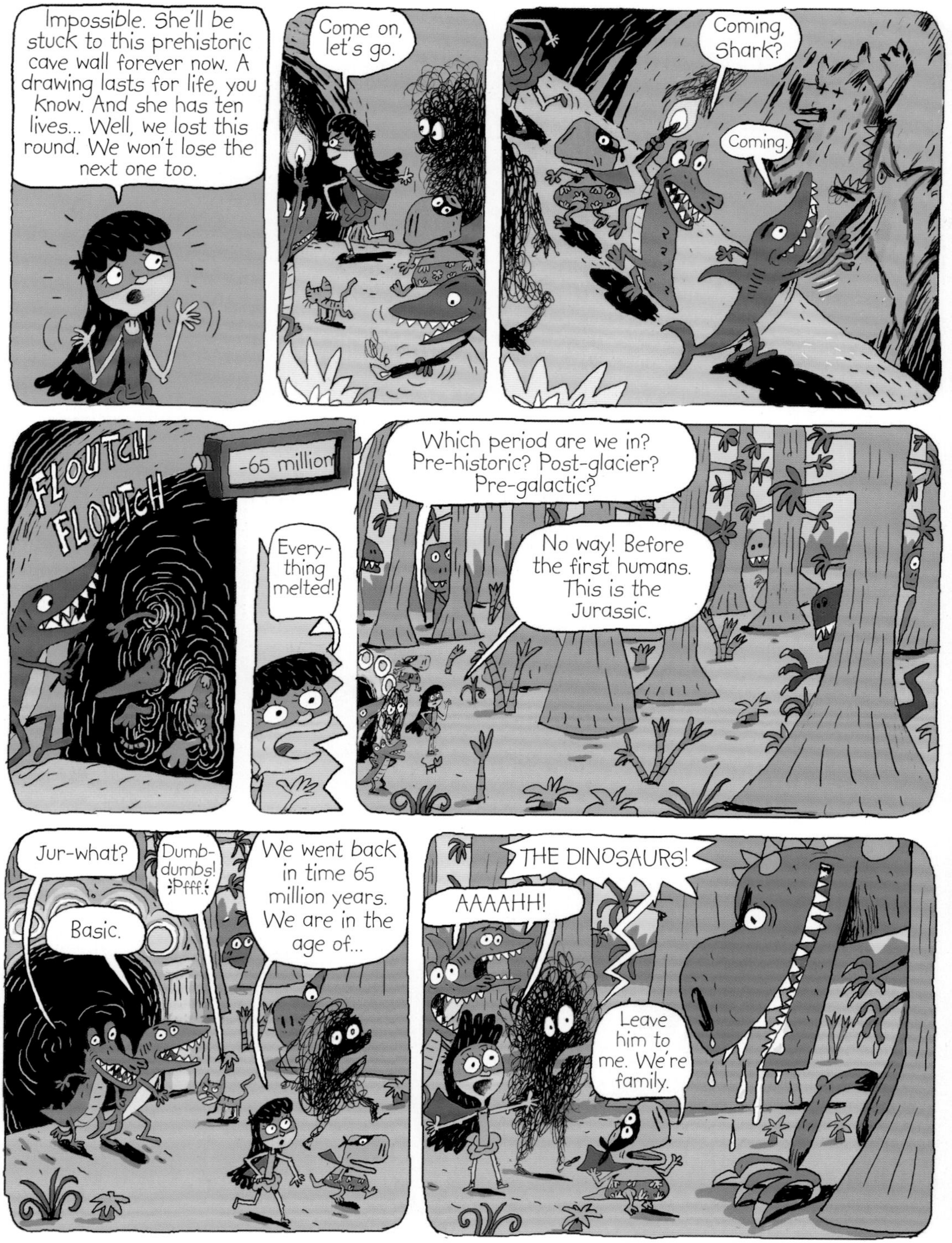
Impossible. She'll be stuck to this prehistoric cave wall forever now. A drawing lasts for life, you know. And she has ten lives... Well, we lost this round. We won't lose the next one too.
Come on, let's go.
Coming, Shark?
Coming.
FLOUTCH FLOUTCH
-65 million
Every-thing melted!
Which period are we in? Pre-historic? Post-glacier? Pre-galactic?
No way! Before the first humans. This is the Jurassic.
Jur-what?
Basic.
Dumb-dumbs! Pfff.
We went back in time 65 million years. We are in the age of...
THE DINOSAURS!
AAAAHH!
Leave him to me. We're family.

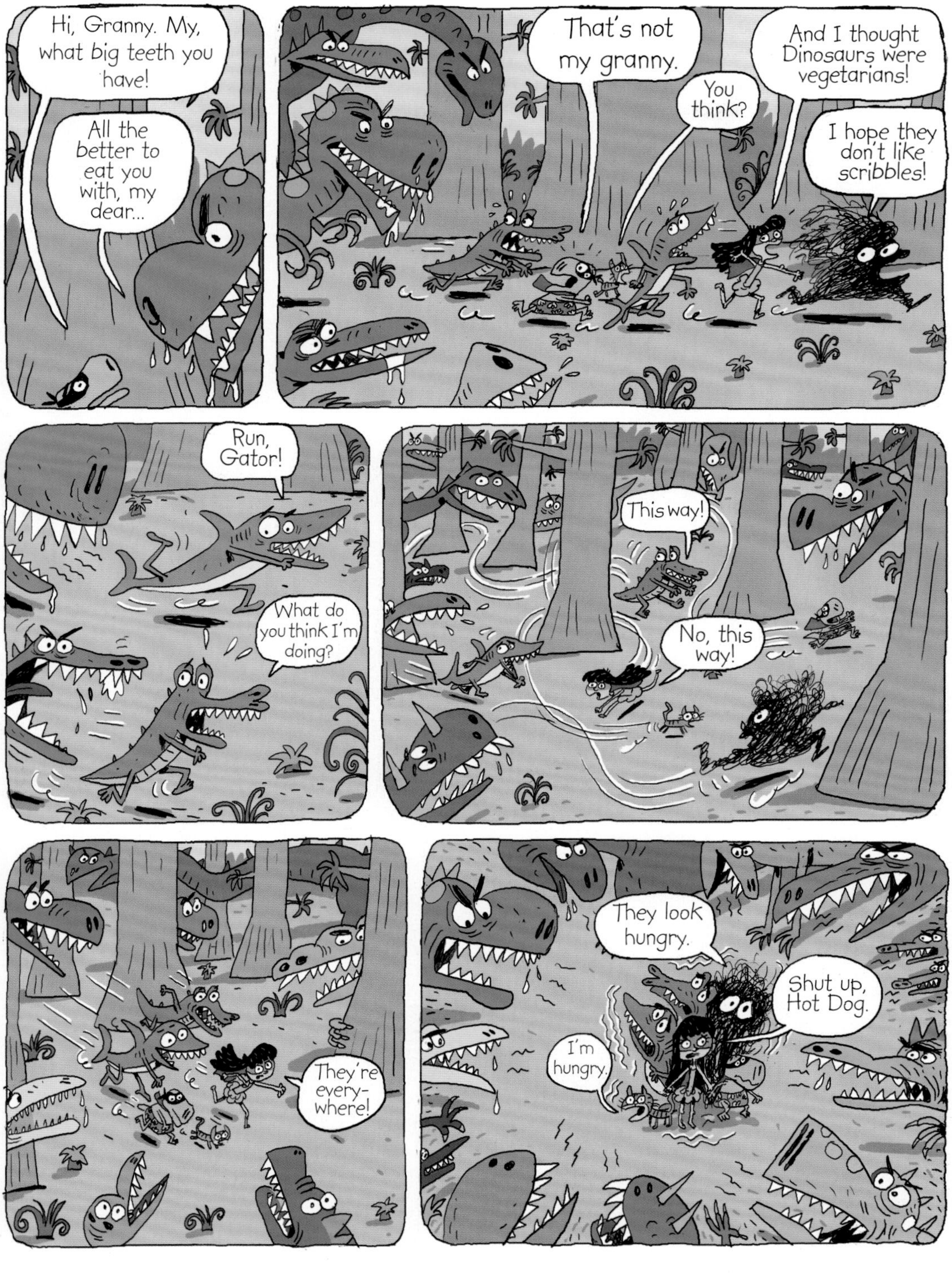

Hi, Granny. My, what big teeth you have!
All the better to eat you with, my dear...
That's not my granny.
You think?
And I thought Dinosaurs were vegetarians!
I hope they don't like scribbles!
Run, Gator!
What do you think I'm doing?
This way!
No, this way!
They're every-where!
They look hungry.
Shut up, Hot Dog.
I'm hungry.

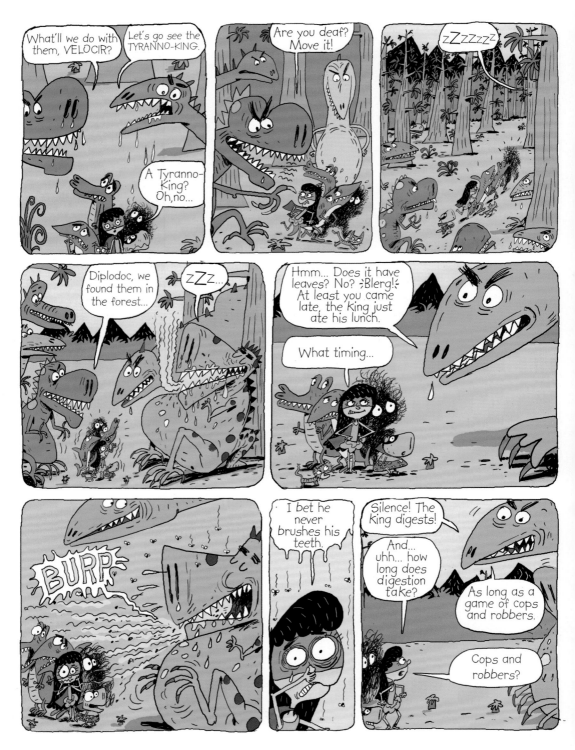

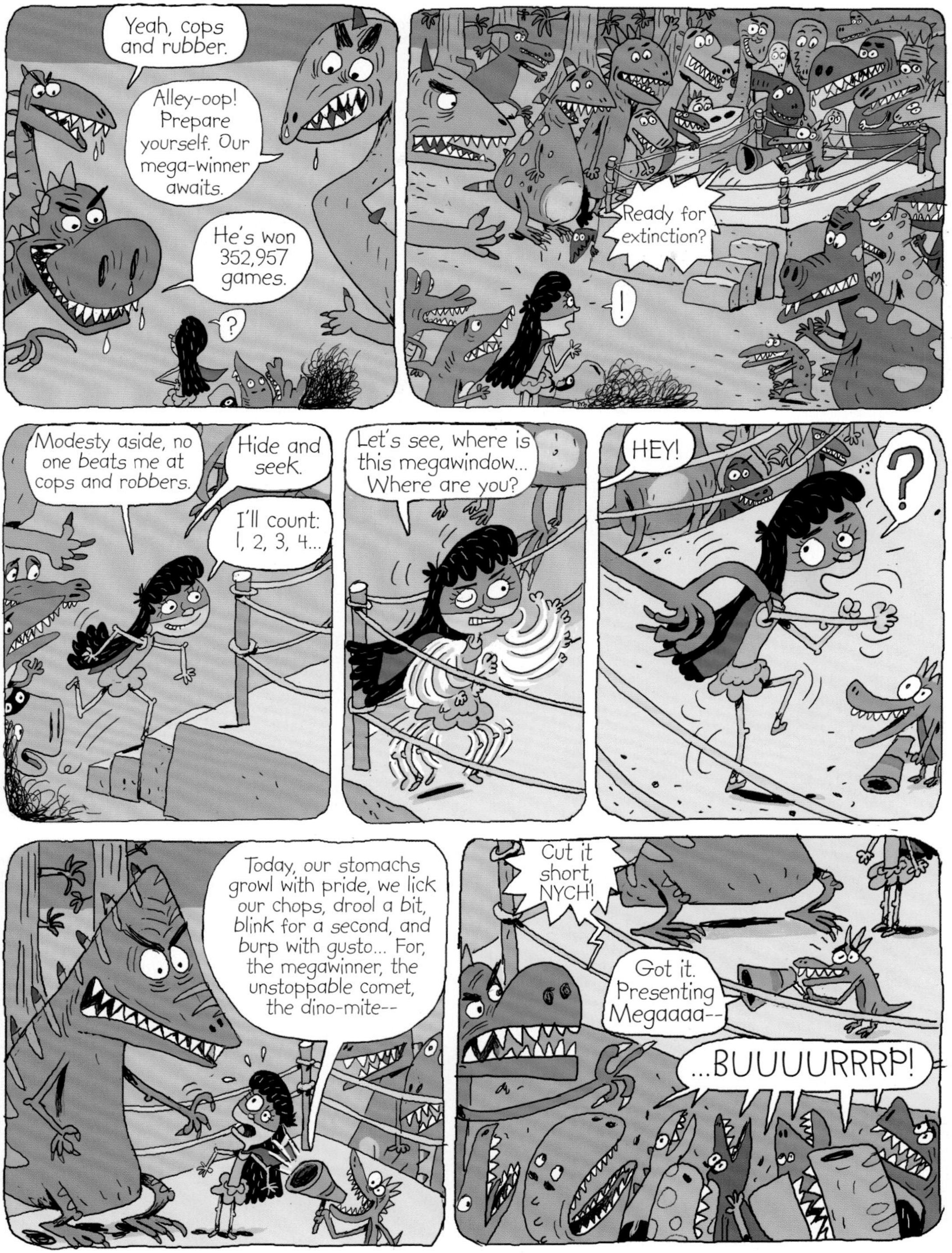
Yeah, cops and rubber.
Alley-oop! Prepare yourself. Our mega-winner awaits.
He's won 352,957 games.
?
Ready for extinction?
!
Modesty aside, no one beats me at cops and robbers.
Hide and seek.
I'll count: 1, 2, 3, 4...
Let's see, where is this megawindow... Where are you?
HEY!
?
Today, our stomachs growl with pride, we lick our chops, drool a bit, blink for a second, and burp with gusto... For, the megawinner, the unstoppable comet, the dino-mite--
Cut it short, NYCH!
Got it. Presenting Megaaaa--
...BUUUURRRP!

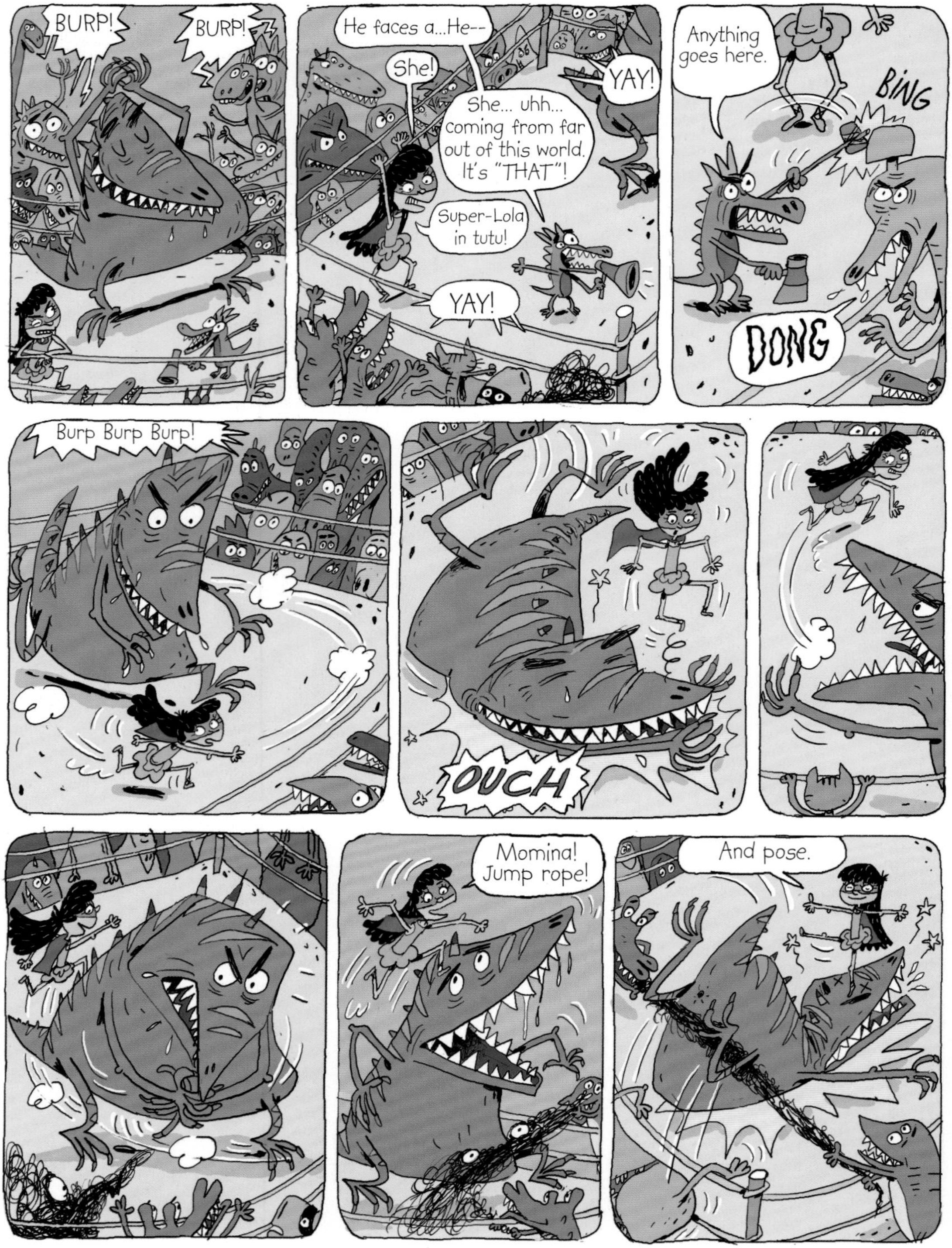
BURP!
BURP!
He faces a...He--
She!
She... uhh... coming from far out of this world. It's "THAT"!
YAY!
Super-Lola in tutu!
YAY!
Anything goes here.
BING
DONG
Burp Burp Burp!
OUCH
Momina! Jump rope!
And pose.

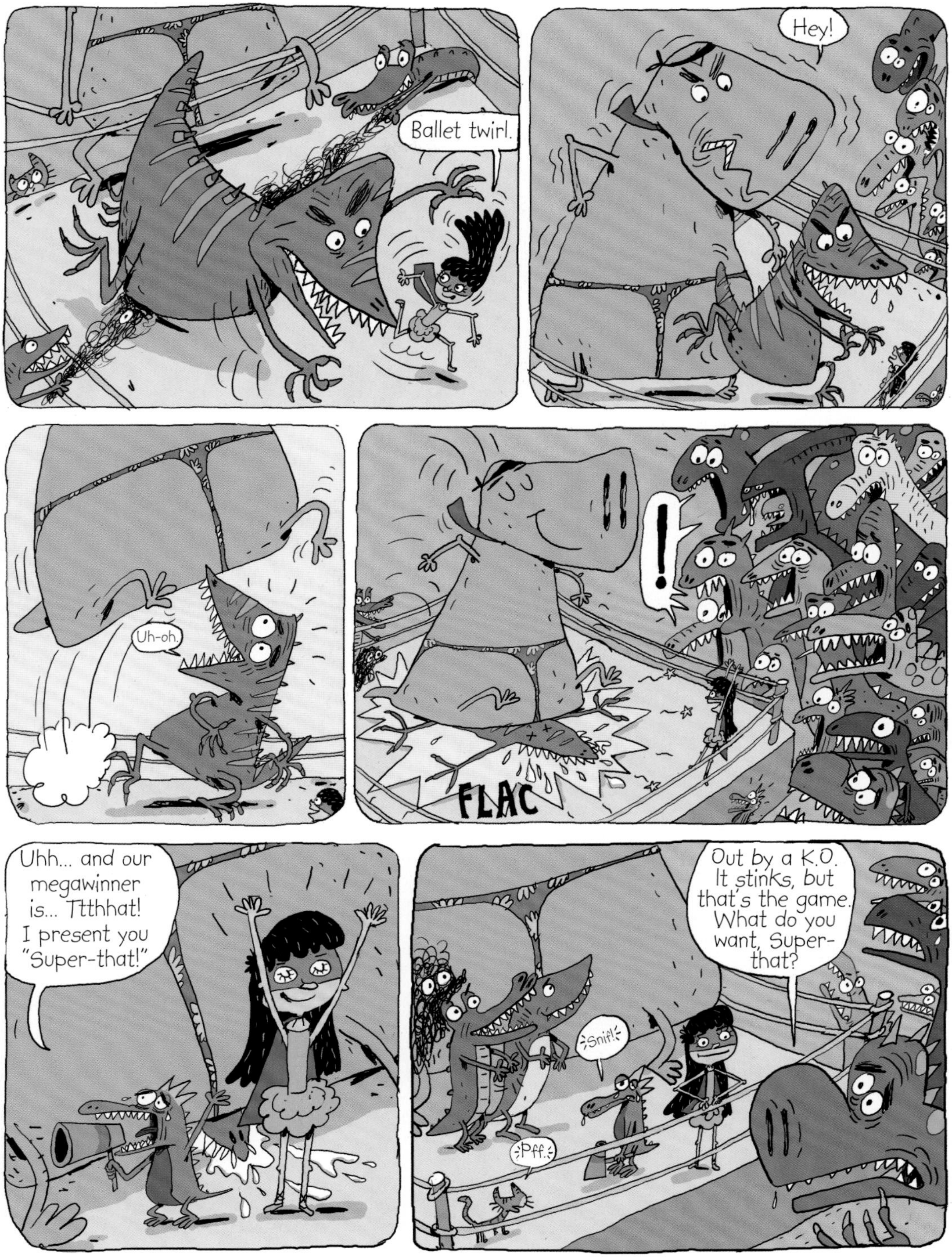
Ballet twirl.
Hey!
Uh-oh.
!
FLAC
Uhh... and our megawinner is... Ttthhat! I present you "Super-that!"
Out by a K.O. It stinks, but that's the game. What do you want, Super-that?
Snif!
Pff.

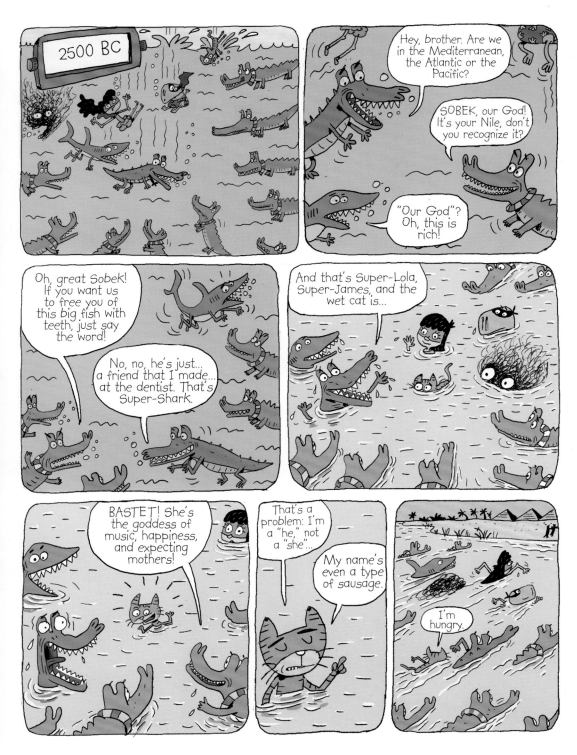

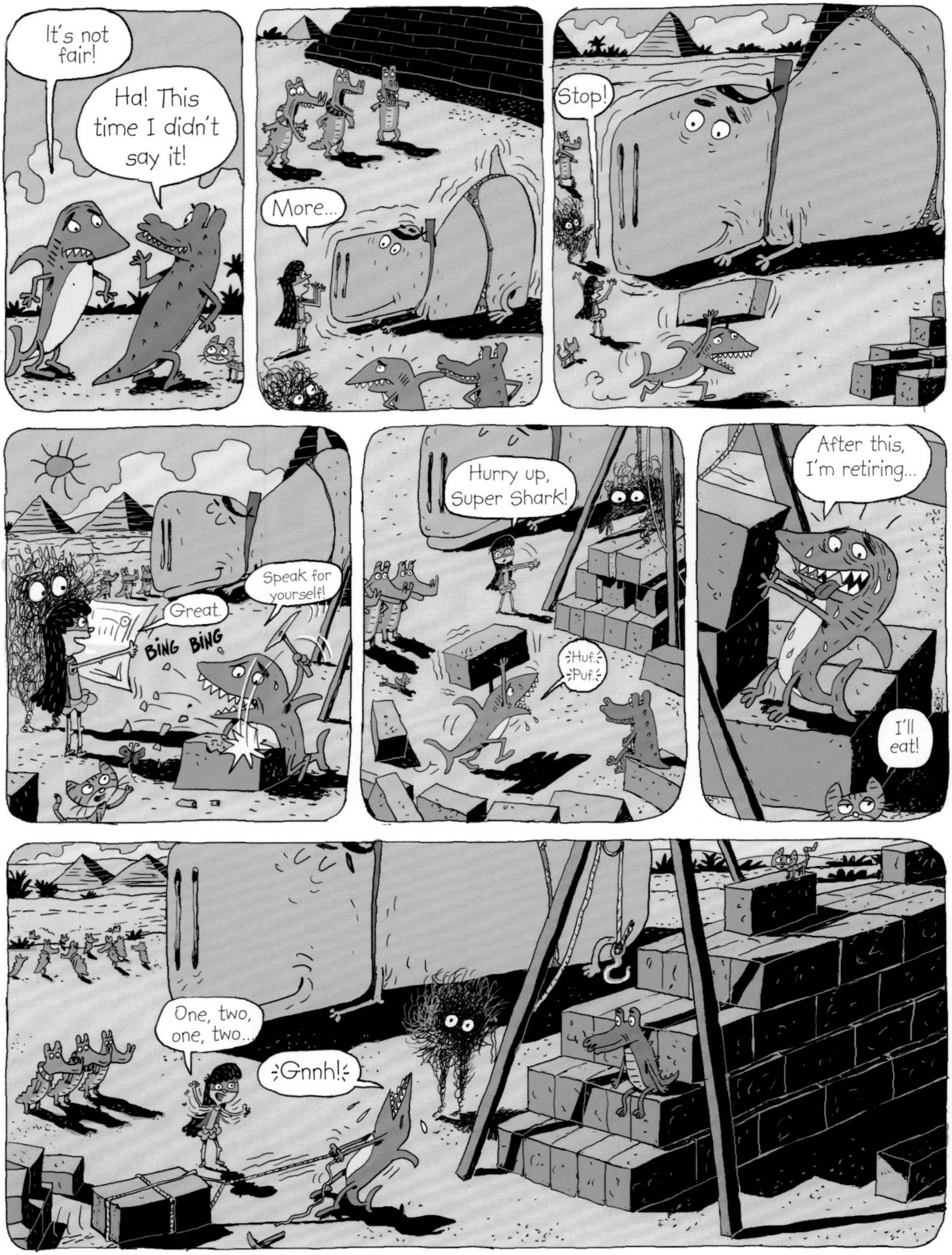
It's not fair!
Ha! This time I didn't say it!
More...
Stop!
Great.
Speak for yourself!
BING BING
Hurry up, Super Shark!
Huf. Puf.
After this, I'm retiring...
I'll eat!
One, two, one, two...
Gnnh!

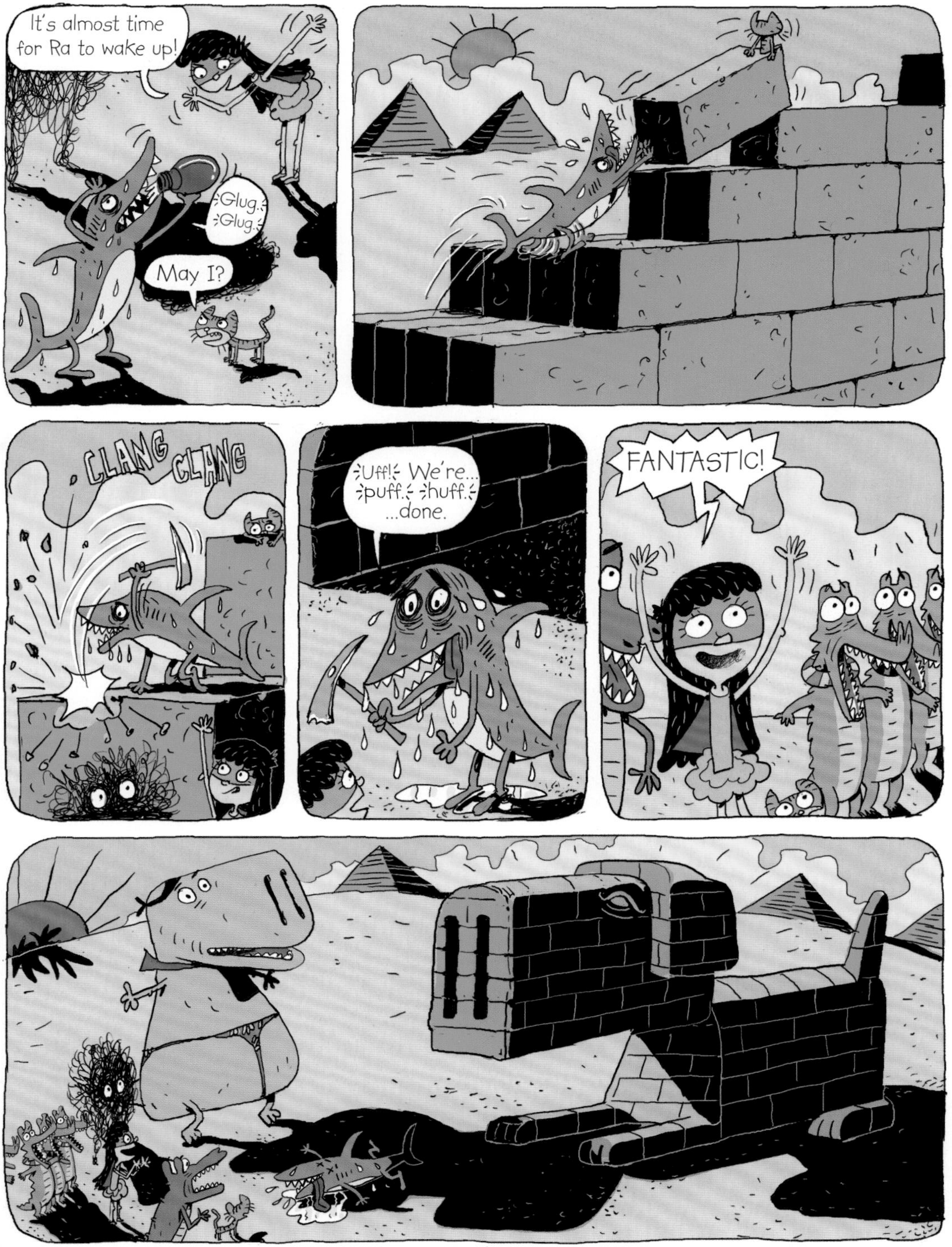
It's almost time for Ra to wake up!
Glug. Glug.
May I?
CLANG CLANG
Uff! We're... puff. huff. ...done.
FANTASTIC!

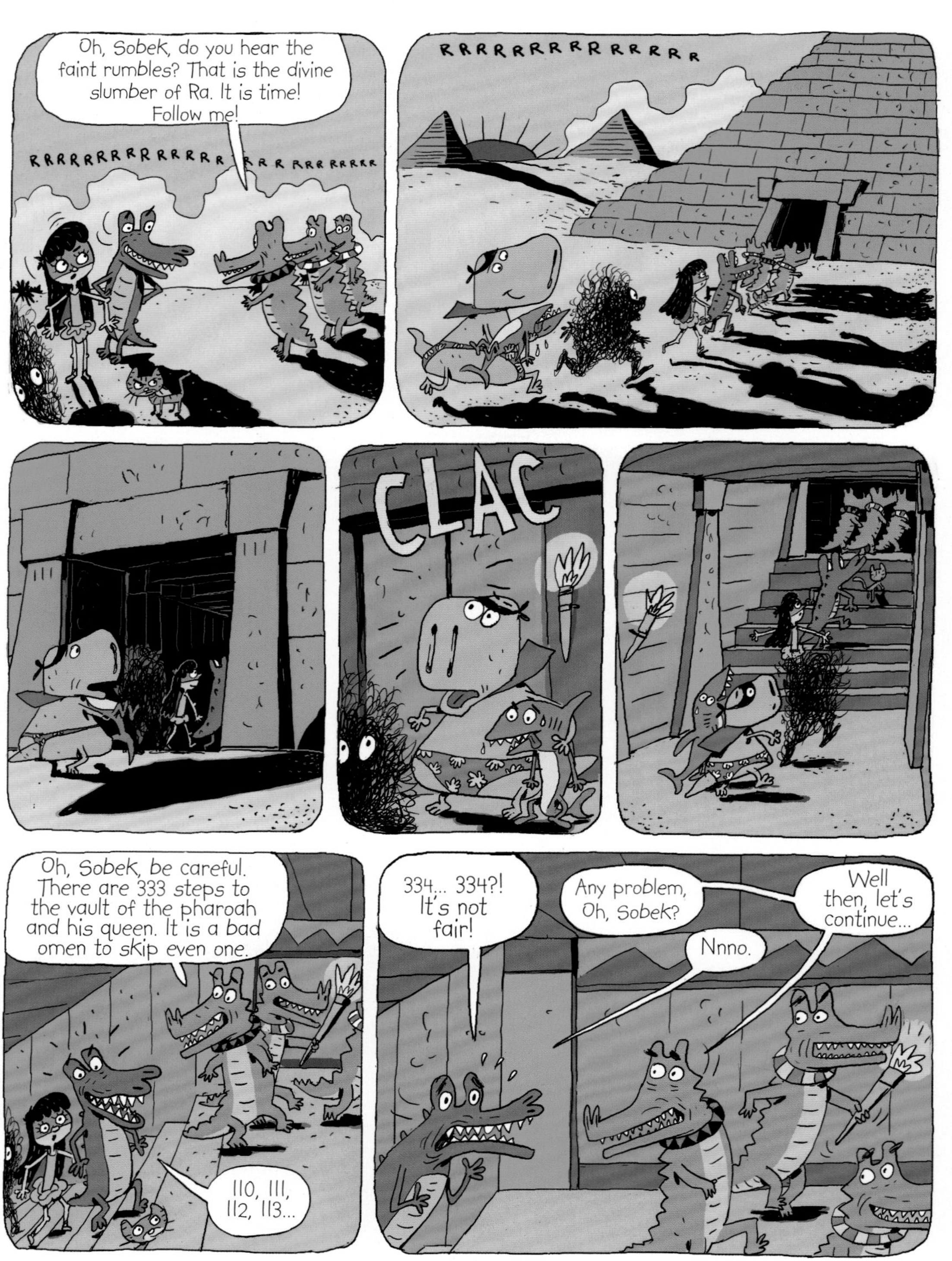

Oh, Sobek, do you hear the faint rumbles? That is the divine slumber of Ra. It is time! Follow me!
RRRRRRRRRRRRRRRRRRRRRRRRRRRRR
RRRRRRRRRRRRRRR
CLAC
Oh, Sobek, be careful. There are 333 steps to the vault of the pharoah and his queen. It is a bad omen to skip even one.
110, 111, 112, 113...
334... 334?! It's not fair!
Any problem, Oh, Sobek?
Nnno.
Well then, let's continue...

77

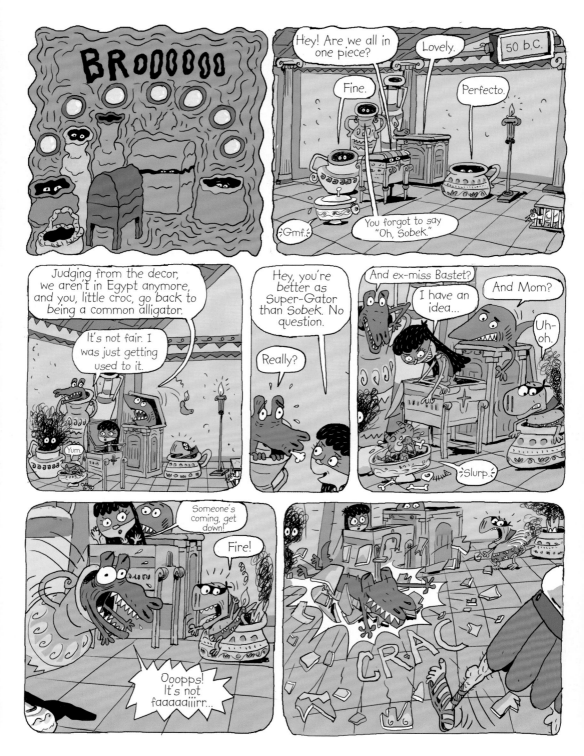

80

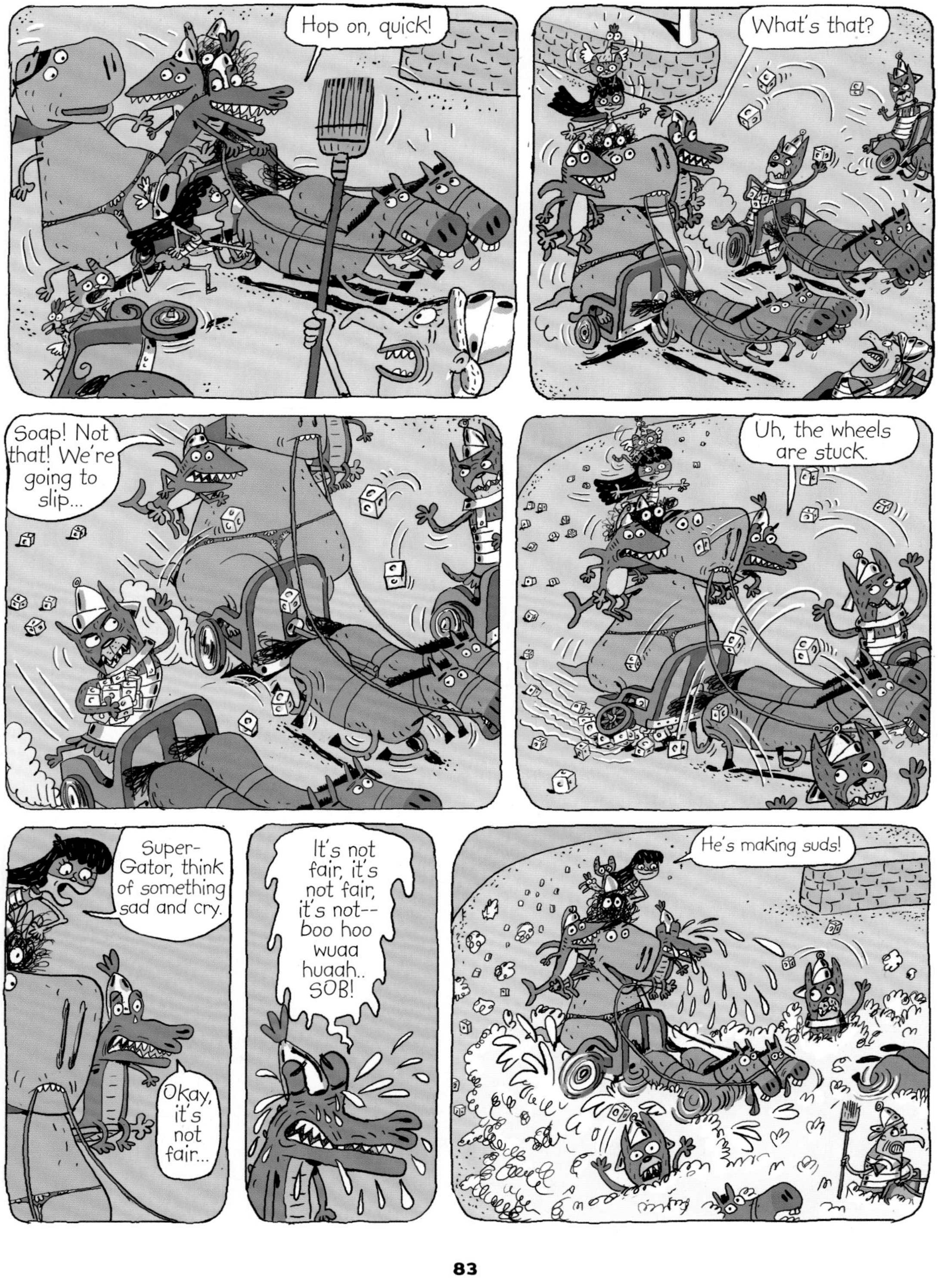
Hop on, quick!
What's that?
Soap! Not that! We're going to slip...
Uh, the wheels are stuck.
Super-Gator, think of something sad and cry.
Okay, it's not fair...
It's not fair, it's not fair, it's not-- boo hoo wuaa huaah.. SOB!
He's making suds!

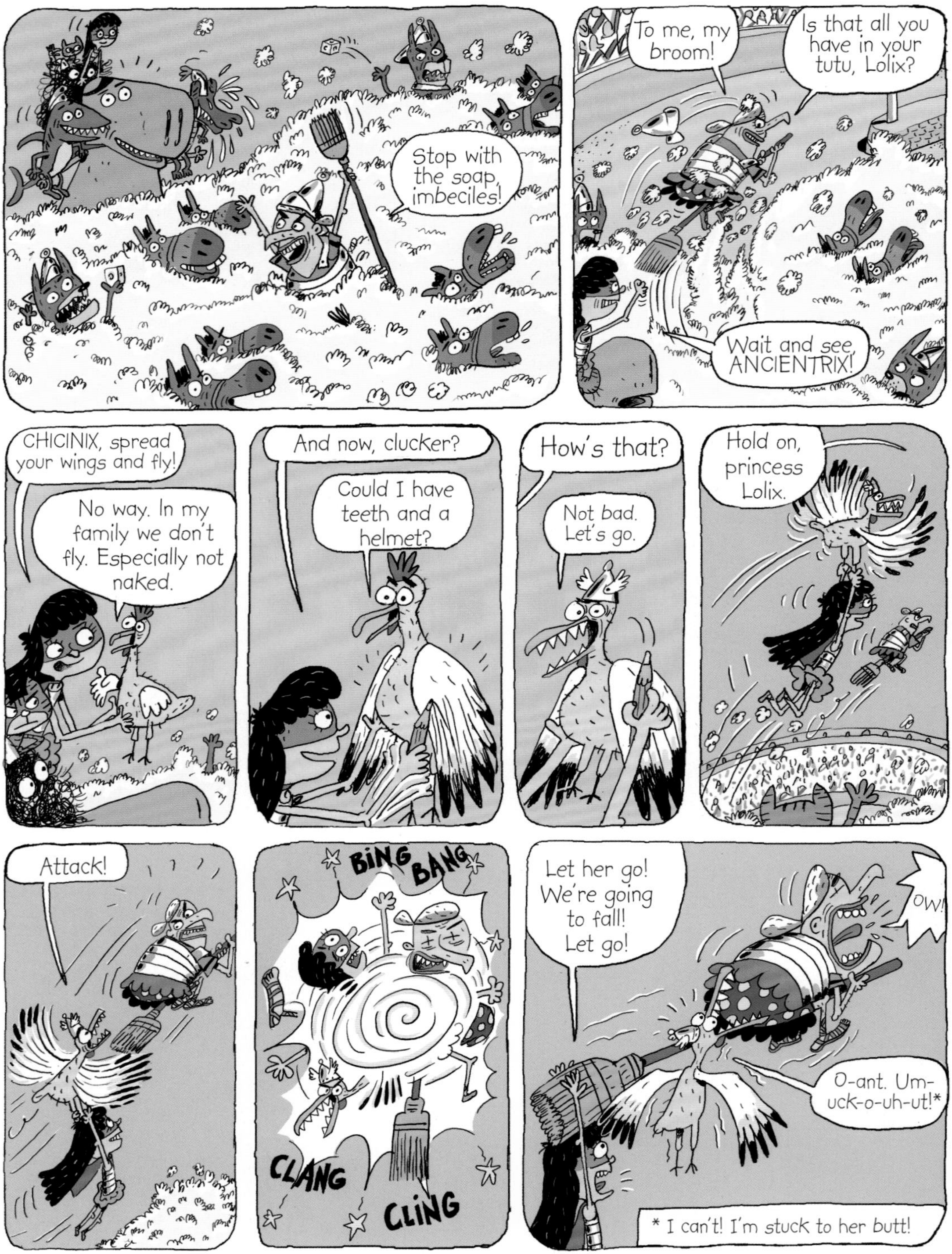

Stop with the soap, imbeciles!
To me, my broom!
Is that all you have in your tutu, Lolix?
Wait and see, ANCIENTRIX!
CHICINIX, spread your wings and fly!
No way. In my family we don't fly. Especially not naked.
And now, clucker?
Could I have teeth and a helmet?
How's that?
Not bad. Let's go.
Hold on, princess Lolix.
Attack!
BING
BANG
CLANG
CLING
Let her go! We're going to fall! Let go!
OW!
O-ant. Um-uck-o-uh-ut!*
* I can't! I'm stuck to her butt!

85

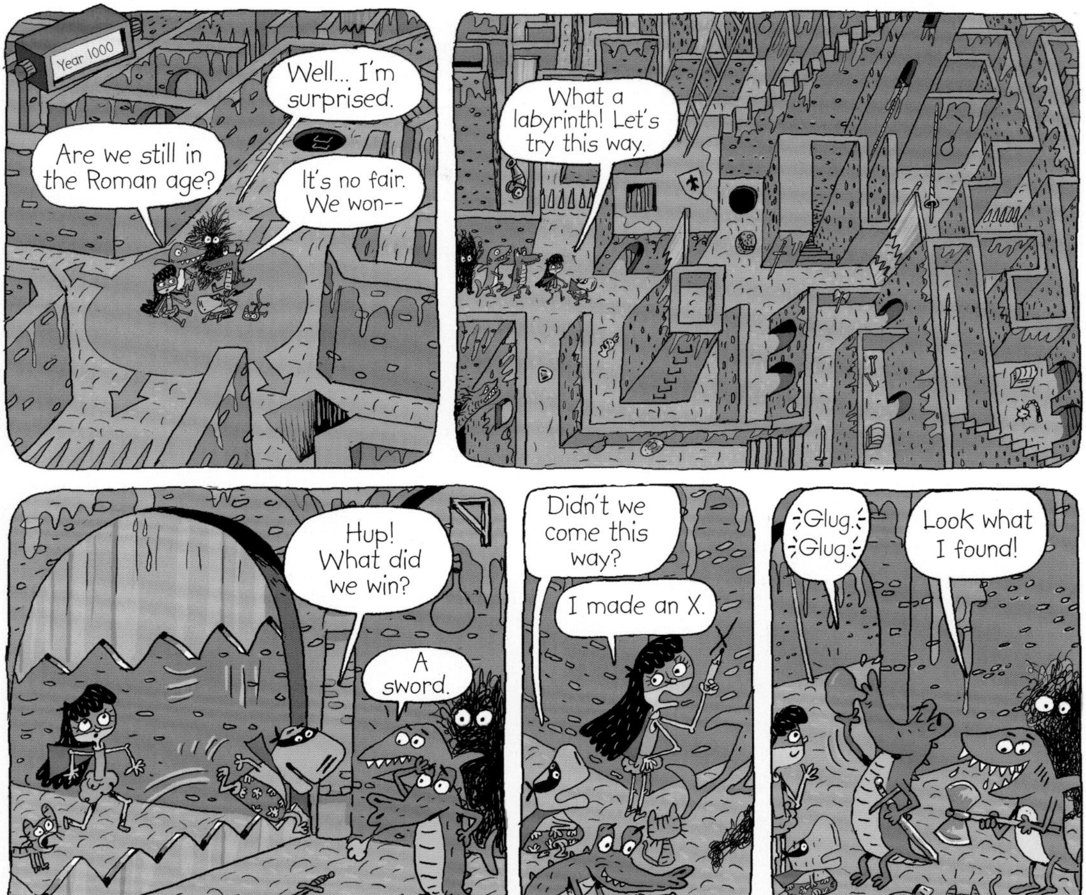
Year 1000
Are we still in the Roman age?
Well... I'm surprised.
It's no fair. We won--
What a labyrinth! Let's try this way.
Hup! What did we win?
A sword.
Didn't we come this way?
I made an X.
Glug. Glug.
Look what I found!
There's 3 X's here.
And bones...
Think we made it to the present day?
Do modern day skeletons have armor?
Come on, we haven't tried that door yet...

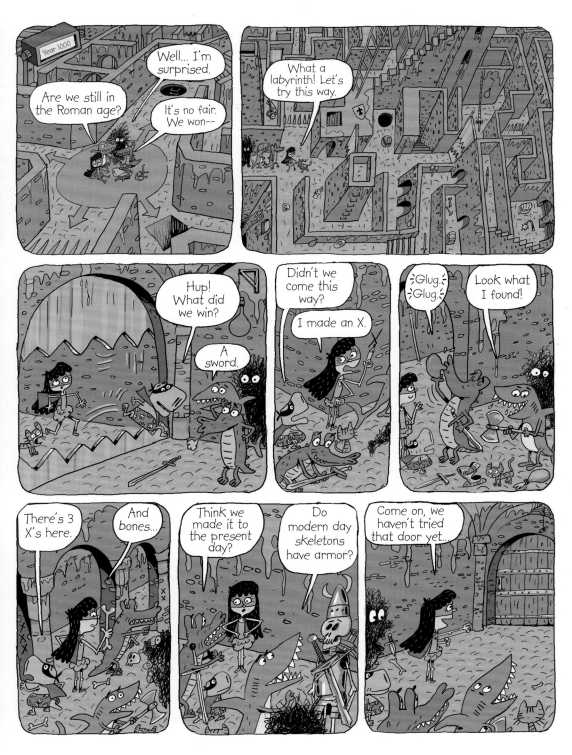

89

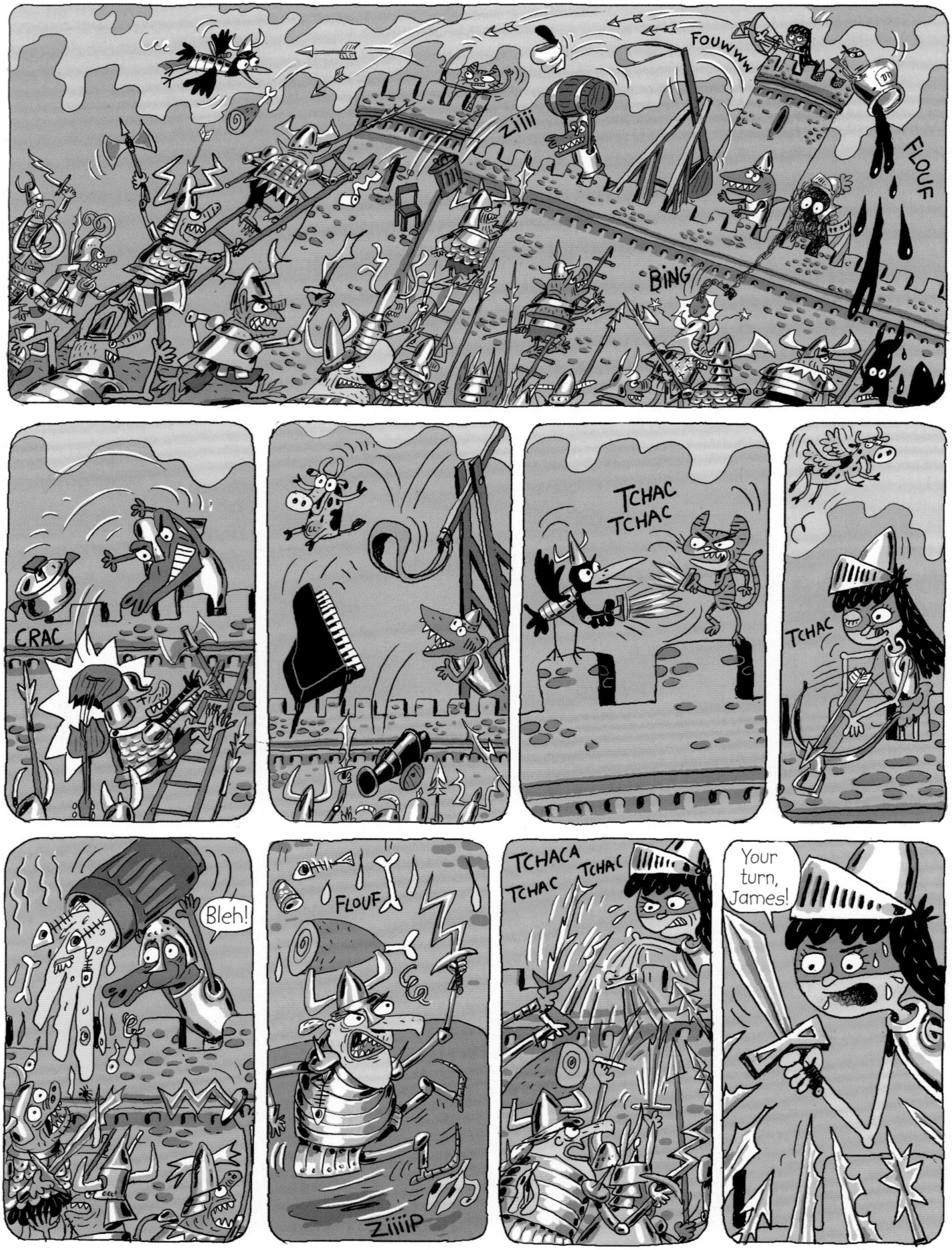
FOUWWW
ZIIII
FLOUF
BING
CRAC
TCHAC
TCHAC
TCHAC
Bleh!
FLOUF
ZIIIIP
TCHACA
TCHAC
TCHAC
Your turn, James!

94

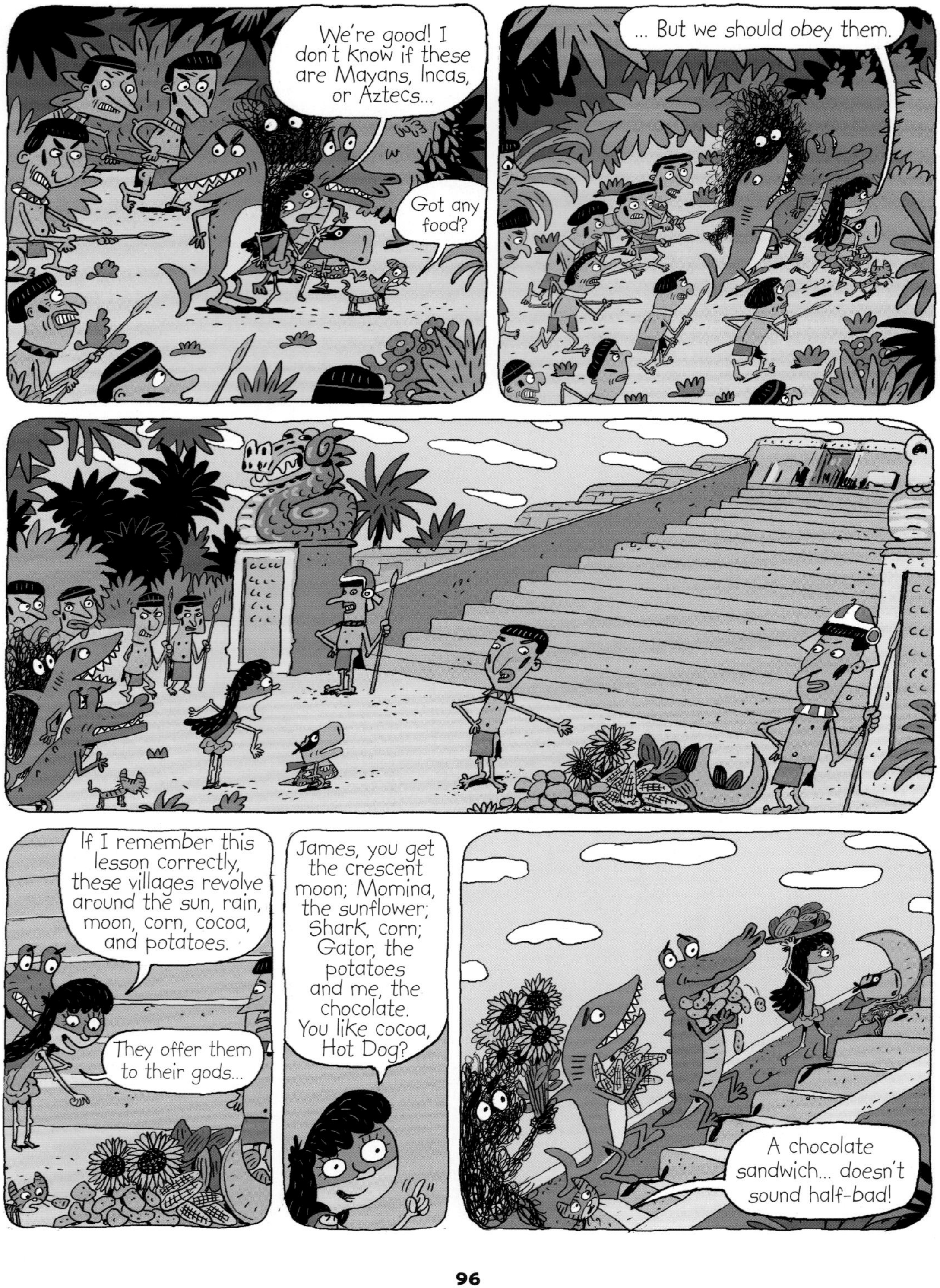
We're good! I don't know if these are Mayans, Incas, or Aztecs...
Got any food?
... But we should obey them.
If I remember this lesson correctly, these villages revolve around the sun, rain, moon, corn, cocoa, and potatoes.
They offer them to their gods...
James, you get the crescent moon; Momina, the sunflower; Shark, corn; Gator, the potatoes and me, the chocolate. You like cocoa, Hot Dog?
A chocolate sandwich... doesn't sound half-bad!

WATCH OUT FOR PAPERCUT

Welcome to LOLA'S SUPER CLUB #1 "My Dad is a Super Secret Agent," by Christine Beigel and Pierre Fouillet, from Papercutz—those mere mortals dedicated to publishing great graphic novels for all ages. I'm Jim Salicrup, the Editor-in-Chief and person who is about to tell you about some Papercutz graphic novels you may enjoy if you loved LOLA'S SUPER CLUB…

But first we must ask ourselves, is Lola a true super-hero or just a girl with a very active imagination? If you believe Lola and her friends are the real deal, you might really like THE MYTHICS, the Papercutz graphic novel series about six children who are called upon by their god-like ancestors to battle an ancient evil that has returned to Earth. In THE MYTHICS #1 "Heroes Reborn," by Patrick Sobral, Patricia Lyfoung, Philippe Ogaki, Jenny, and Dara, you'll meet the first three of the six heroes: Yuko, a Japanese schoolgirl in a rock band, who has electrical powers; Amir, a recently-orphaned young Egyptian boy who must take over his family's successful business, whose powers are derived from the sun and the moon; and a young opera hopeful, Abigail, whose voice also becomes her super power. These children all suddenly find themselves in unreal situations, granted great powers, and having to battle powerful foes to save their cities. Hey, it's not always fun and games being a super-hero. Spoiler Alert: Quetzalcoatl, who we see on page 97, appears in THE MYTHICS #2.

But if you think Lola's adventures are just imaginary tales she dreams up, you may also enjoy THE SISTERS by Cazenove and William, the Papercutz graphic novel series about Wendy and Maureen, who lead fairly ordinary lives driving each other crazy, but then they also imagine themselves as the Super Sisters and have all sorts of real-life inspired adventures. These mini-adventures are so popular within their already super popular series, that an entire graphic novel has been created by Cazenove and William devoted exclusively to their super-hero fantasies, Naturally it's called THE SUPER SISTERS, and there's a super-secret sneak peek of one of the stories in a few pages…

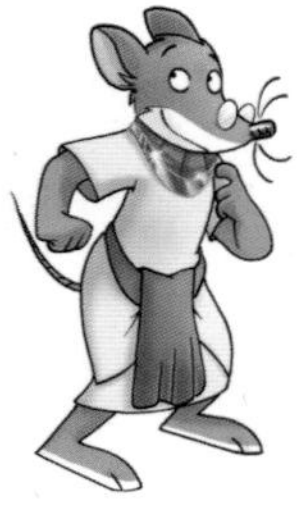

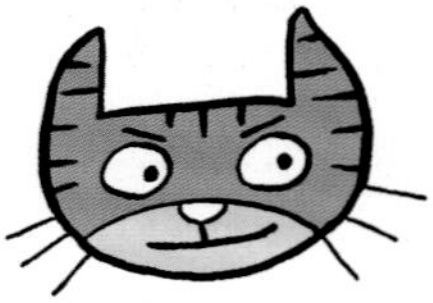

There's also another aspect of Lola's adventures that we witnessed in the second story in this graphic novel, that's where Lola and her super-friends travel through time. This is a very popular concept in several Papercutz graphic novel series. Perhaps our most experienced time-traveler is Geronimo Stilton, the editor-in-chief of the *Rodent's Gazette*. Geronimo has hopped in the Speedrat countless times to save the future, by protecting the past from his enemies, the Pirate Cats. Oh, in case you didn't know, Geronimo's a mouse. The talking kind who lives in New Mouse City. Yet his world is remarkably similar to ours, especially regarding major historic events. It's just a lot mousier. Check out the special excerpt from GERONOMO STILTON #2 starting on page 109.

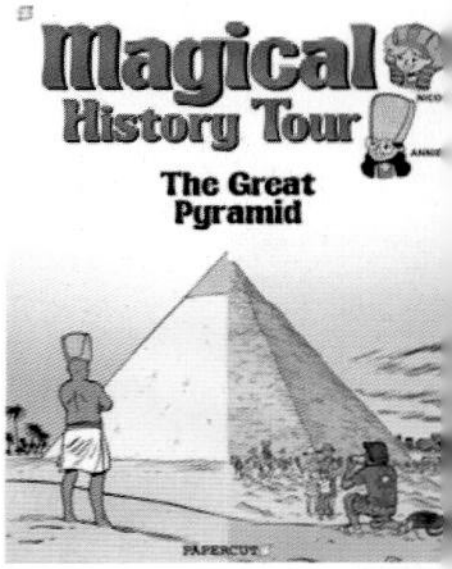
Magical History Tour
NICO
ANNIE
The Great Pyramid
PAPERCUTZ

For a somewhat more human experience through time, may we suggest the premiere volume of the newest Papercutz graphic novel series, MAGICAL HISTORY TOUR #1 "The Great Pyramid" by Fabrice Erre and Sylvain Savoia? Within its pages Nico and Annie will be your guide through important events in history. Usually each volume focuses on one major event or time period and their aren't any nasty super-villains trying to disrupt everything. And unlike Lola's rushed trip through time, in this series you get to linger a bit.

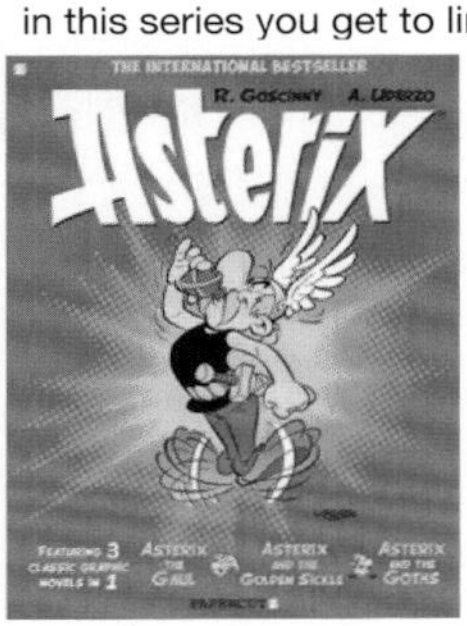
THE INTERNATIONAL BESTSELLER
R. GOSCINNY A. UDERZO
ASTERIX
FEATURING 3 CLASSIC GRAPHIC NOVELS IN 1
ASTERIX THE GAUL
ASTERIX AND THE GOLDEN SICKLE
ASTERIX AND THE GOTHS
PAPERCUTZ

When Lola landed in 50 BC, some of you may have gotten the inside gags based on one of the best-selling comics series in the world, ASTERIX. That's the comic Lola refers to when she says "to defeat the Romans you must drink a magic potion." If you're not already a fan of ASTERIX, the little Gaul who gains super-strength from a magic potion that helps him battle the Romans, then you're in luck! Papercutz has recently started publishing all new translations of the classic comics series by Goscinny and Uderzo, and it's your opportunity to not only meet the real "Dogmatix," but to experience one of the greatest graphic novel series ever created.

We saved the best news for last. I'm happy to announce you are now officially a member of LOLA'S SUPER CLUB! As you know the membership requirements are super-tough: you have to have either a super power or an imagination. You know what you have. We hope you enjoyed LOLA'S SUPER CLUB #1 and that you'll be back for #2 "My Substitute Teacher is a Witch," as it won't be any fun without you!

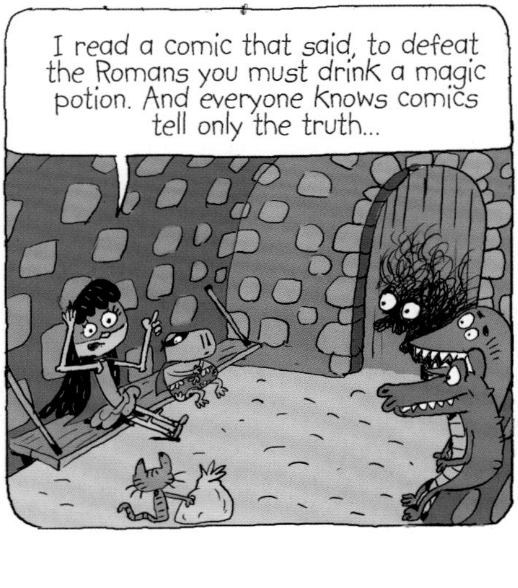
I read a comic that said, to defeat the Romans you must drink a magic potion. And everyone knows comics tell only the truth...

Thanks!

Jim

STAY IN TOUCH!

EMAIL: salicrup@papercutz.com
WEB: papercutz.com
TWITTER: @papercutzgn
INSTAGRAM: @papercutzgn
FACEBOOK: PAPERCUTZGRAPHICNOVELS
FAN MAIL: Papercutz, 160 Broadway, Suite 700, East Wing New York, NY 10038

THE ALIENS HAD BURST ONTO ASTERIA WITHOUT ADVANCE WARNING. LUCKILY WE SUPER SISTERS WERE THERE TO DEFEND OUR FRIENDS.

HEEEY! DON'T YOU GET THE FEELING I'M STUCK DOING ALL THE WORK?!

WELL, YEAH. BUT GIVEN THAT I CAN'T DO A THING...

YES, WELL, IT'S STILL NOT MY FAULT IF---

BAF

CRAK

BAM

...I WAS SAYING, IT'S NOT MY FAULT IF MY LASER'S THE ONLY ONE THAT CAN DESTROY THEM.

WZAP

WZAP

YOU'VE GOT TWO MORE BEHIND YOU.

THE SISTERS, SUPER SISTERS by Cazenove and William © 2020 Bamboo Édition

Will Maureen master her powers or just blow everything up? Find out in THE SUPER SISTERS available now wherever books are sold.

Catch a ride to Ancient Egypt with GERONIMO STILTON in this special excerpt of GERONIMO STILTON #2 "The Secret of the Sphinx"...

HEY, WHAT'S IT GOT TO DO WITH ME?

YOU'RE THE ONE WHO REPRO-GRAMMED THE COMPUTER BECAUSE YOU WANTED TO STOP OFF IN THE MIDDLE AGES... FOR A SNACK!

-≥TSK≤-... MAYBE IT HAPPENED WHEN YOU HOPPED AROUND ALL OVER THE PLACE JUST BECAUSE I TICKLED YOU!

IT'S NOT MY FAULT I'M TICKLISH!

THE FACT REMAINS THAT WE NOW FIND OURSELVES IN A DESERT MORE DESERTED THAN THE SAHARA!

!

WELL, MAYBE IT'S NOT QUITE THAT DESERTED! *LOOK!*

ROTTEN ROQUEFORT! *A PYRAMID!*

IT'S GIGANTIC!

OF COURSE, WE LANDED ON THE *GIZA PLATEAU!* THIS HAS TO BE THE PYRAMID OF CHEOPS!

GIZA PLATEAU
NORTH OF MEMPHIS, IT WAS CHOSEN BY THE PHARAOH CHEOPS, CHEPHREN'S FATHER, AS THE SITE FOR HIS OWN PYRAMID. AT 480 FEET IN HEIGHT AND 656 FEET ALONG EACH SIDE AT THE BASE, THE PYRAMID OF CHEOPS IS THE LARGEST PYRAMID IN ANCIENT EGYPT. IT TOOK OVER 20 YEARS TO BUILD AND MORE THAN 2,000,000 BLOCKS OF STONE THAT WEIGHED AROUND 2.5 TONS EACH. THE PYRAMIDS OF CHEPHREN, HIS SON MICERINO, AND THE SPHINX WERE ALSO BUILT AT GIZA.

Unearth more historical findings with Geronimo and friends in GERONIMO STILTON #2 "The Secret of the Sphinx" available wherever fine books are sold.